THE BEARS UPSTAIRS

The Bears Upstairs

BY DOROTHY HAAS

A YEARLING BOOK

Published by
Dell Publishing Co., Inc.
1 Dag Hammarskjold Plaza
New York, New York 10017

Yearling ® TM 913705, Dell Publishing Co., Inc.

ISBN: 0-440-40448-7

Reprinted by arrangement with Greenwillow Books (a division of
William Morrow & Company, Inc.)

Printed in the United States of America

First Yearling printing—March 1981

CW

Chapter 1

Wendy really wasn't supposed to be downstairs in the lobby at that hour. Her mother had said more than once that she wished Wendy would stay upstairs in the apartment at least until after breakfast for heaven's sake. But it was a good thing Wendy was exactly where she was this rainy October day. Otherwise she would have missed the most exciting thing ever to happen at the Heywood Arms.

Nobody was around. It was only twenty minutes before seven. Joe the doorman wasn't on duty yet, and it was too early for people in the building to be going through the lobby on their way to work.

The lobby. It was small but elegant. Comfortable gold velvet chairs and Louis XV tables were scattered over the thick, scarlet carpeting. Two shiny-leaved lemon trees in heavy gold pots guarded the entrance. Overhead, a thousand crystal drops spilled from a glittering chandelier.

Wendy was curled up in one of the chairs, contentedly watching the rain, a small figure with honey-hued hair pulled back into a single thick braid that fell nearly to her waist. Her eyes, the deep blue of sky at the edge of night, looked out at the world through gold-rimmed glasses that rode her nose at a skewed angle.

It can be a cozy thing, watching the rain when you're indoors and all warm and dry. Wendy fingered the end of her braid and admired the fat drops that bounced on the sidewalk on either side of the awning that led away from the glass doors, over the drive, out to the street. The place under the awning was dry. But the street was rain shiny and the trees and the big old houses across the way were reflected in the wetness —wavery, upside-down pictures from where she sat.

She was thinking how really great it would be if everything could be shiny like that all the time, even in good weather, when a yellow taxi turned into the drive and stopped under the awning. A smallish, round-ish person climbed out.

Wendy had never seen anyone dressed like this before. Her eyes widened. She pushed her glasses higher on her nose and pulled herself up onto her knees, staring.

The little person was enveloped in a long, red-and-black plaid coat. Above the coat was a floppy red hat trimmed with a stick-up flower and wound round with a filmy red scarf. Wendy squinted, trying to see the face behind the scarf. She couldn't. It was exactly like trying to see into a house through curtains. Someone inside might be able to look out through the window, but nobody outside could see in.

The strange little person reached into the cab and hauled out a quaint old hump-shaped suitcase, the kind that used to be called a valise. She set it gently on the ground. And then another figure emerged from the cab. He was dressed even more oddly than his friend.

His coat was long and fuzzy and white, striped around the middle in red and yellow and green and black. Just like Grandma Cheever's Hudson Bay blanket, Wendy thought in startled recognition. The collar of the coat was turned up to meet the broad brim of a white cowboy hat.

Wendy craned her neck, trying to see the face under the hat. It wasn't possible.

The oblong leather suitcases the visitor took from the cab were as old-fashioned as the valise, bound with leather straps and wrapped with prickly looking rope. His shoulders sagged when he lifted the suitcases, but he handled them carefully, avoiding a pillar as he turned toward the entrance.

The cab drove away with a great squishing and splashing, and the visitors stood looking up at the highrises that lined Sheridan Road at the corner. Wendy bounced out of her chair and ran to hold the door. She backed through it, bumping, and stood waiting for them to come inside.

As one, they turned. Wendy felt herself being studied by two pairs of eyes she couldn't see. The moment was endless.

Then, "Good mor-r-rning, child." The voice from under the cowboy hat was deep, rich, and mellow, with a curious roughening of the *r*'s. He set down the suitcases and Wendy became aware of his hands.

His hands! Were they "furry"? Were they *hands* at all? She shivered, caught her breath, stepped backward, letting the door close part way. The lobby behind her, though its walls were mostly glass, seemed suddenly as safe as a fortress. A part of her wanted to run inside and bolt the door. But Wendy tried never to let herself get away with being scared. If she was afraid of something, she usually walked right up to it and made it go away. And besides—now she was curious. She wanted to know more about these outlandish visitors to the Heywood.

A furry paw—it was a paw!—reached up and lifted the cowboy hat slightly. The bear who wore it bowed.

"I am called Otto." He broke the word in two. Ot-to.

Briefly Wendy looked into a friendly, furry face. The mouth tipped up at the corners as though it was used to doing that a lot, and there were laugh crinkles at the corners of eyes that were, astonishingly, as blue as her own.

The bear called Otto smiled at her before resettling

4

his hat, and Wendy knew she had nothing to fear. This was a very pleasant bear.

Nobody had ever bowed to Wendy before, and she wasn't quite sure what to do about it. Then she remembered a girl in a movie about the olden days, and she curtsied, wishing she were wearing a hoopskirt instead of her old blue corduroy jumper.

"I'm Wendy," she said shyly.

"Ursula Ma'am here, and—" Otto turned to where, moments before, the small creature in the red coat had been standing. The space was empty. Beyond the nearest pillar, reflected in the rain-slicked paving stones, was a splash of red.

Otto spoke gently to the invisible Ursula Ma'am. "Love, it's not to fear. Come. We must go in."

The trembling reply could scarcely be heard above the pattering rain. "It saw us!" There was terror in her words.

Otto's voice was reassuring. "But it's only a small one."

"It could tell the human in charge. We would go in and—and"—the voice quivered— "the human in charge might not let us out."

The meaning of the words dawned on Wendy. She was the "it." They were talking about her! Two bears were standing at the entrance to her very own apartment building and calling her an "it," and one of them was scared of *her!*

"Come and look at its eyes, love." Otto was quietly encouraging. "They are trustworthy eyes. I do not think it would hurt us."

Nobody had ever been afraid of Wendy before. Suddenly she wanted to help the small frightened creature with the soft voice. She stepped outside, still holding the door so it wouldn't close and lock them out, and spoke to the hidden Ursula Ma'am. "Oh, I wouldn't! I won't tell a single soul you're here. Not even Kelly and Sara. I promise."

Silence.

"Cross my heart." Wendy did just that. "Hope to die."

Another pause. The reflection moved. Ursula Ma'am stepped into view. She approached slowly, listing slightly with the weight of the valise, the flower on her hat bobbing.

How do you look trustworthy? How do you look as though a bear can put her faith in you? It was a problem Wendy had never faced before. Her eyes showed worry, if anything.

The red-coated bear stood before her and looked directly into her face for a long moment.

Not knowing what else to do, Wendy bobbed another curtsey.

A long, trembling sigh came from within the depths of the red hat. "Thank you, child," said Ursula Ma'am.

Otto hoisted the roped suitcases. "Come, love," he

urged quietly. "We must go in before other humans see us."

Wendy caught his uneasiness. Hastily she pushed the door wide open and the two improbable guests padded into the lobby of the Heywood.

Otto stopped at the locked glass door that separated the outer lobby from the elevator area. He dug about in his coat pockets, first one, then the other.

Ursula Ma'am, waiting, rested the valise on the floor. She edged a furry foot out from the folds of her coat and stroked the scuffed leather. "The cheerings," she murmured. She seemed to have erased Wendy from her mind. "The dear cheerings." Fear still tinged her voice, and yet the words had a happy sound.

Wendy studied the valise. Ursula Ma'am treated it so tenderly it must hold something very valuable.

"Ah-huh!" Otto held up a ring with two keys on it. He tried one in the door. It didn't fit. The second one did, and he led the way inside. "The other one is for Dr. Corrigan's shelter, then."

"Dr. Corrigan!" Wendy followed them. "But he lives right above us, in twenty-five-oh-two." The mystery was getting bigger and bigger. "Only, well, not exactly. I mean, he's not here right now. He's in Montana or someplace digging up bones and things for the museum."

"The good Dr. Corrigan." Otto spoke absently, inspecting the carved brass doors of the elevators, patting them where doorknobs would be on ordinary doors. "Humans call these elevators. They carry humans up and down. He told us about them. But how do we make them open? He forgot to tell us that, I think."

Wendy pressed the Up button between the elevators. It lit up. "You push the one with the Up arrow when you want to go up. The car comes and the door just opens. That's all."

The numbered floor lights overhead flashed.

17 . . . 16 . . . 15 . . .

They watched the lights flicker from floor to floor. In the elegance of the lobby, the two strangers in their outlandish clothes stood out like sunflowers in a rose garden.

Ursula Ma'am looked around timidly. "Where are all the humans?" She said the word the way Wendy might have said *werewolf*.

Wendy kept her voice gentle. "It's kind of early. I guess it'll be a while before anyone comes downstairs."

12 . . . 11 . . . 10 . . .

Otto pushed his hat back slightly and studied her face. "Child, would you like to come to see us?" he asked.

There was a gasp from Ursula Ma'am.

He turned to her. "It has seen us. And it has promised to keep our secret. We must tell it more." He

8

turned back to Wendy. "Would you like that?"

7 . . . 6 . . . 5 . . .

"Yes!" Go to see them? Bears in her very own apartment building—would she *not* go to see them! "I'll come this afternoon," she offered. "Right after school."

2 . . . 1 . . .

With a metallic sigh the door of the west car slid open.

"After school, then," Otto repeated, and they entered the elevator, settling their luggage at their feet. He pulled a slip of paper from a pocket. Holding it high, next to the buttons, he studied it. "He said to push the one marked like this."

He found the button and pressed it. Exactly at that moment the door behind Wendy opened and Mr. Pick stepped through it. His long raincoat rustled wetly over his saffron-colored jogging clothes, and his tennis shoes squished in the silence. His gaze followed Wendy's into the elevator as the door slid shut.

"Good *heavens*," he said. "*Who* are *they!* Are there no *limits* to the *types* they let *in*to this *build*ing?" Mr. Pick always talked like that, as though he was playing hopscotch, jumping from word to word.

Wendy put on her most innocent look, trying to act as though there was nothing the least bit unusual about the occupants of the elevator now rising to the twenty-fifth floor. "Oh, they're just visitors," she said with elaborate care.

"Visitors *only*, I should *hope*," sniffed Mr. Pick, pressing the elevator button.

Happily Wendy didn't have to comment on that. A raucous buzz flooded the lobby, the intercom signal people upstairs used when they wanted to talk to the doorman. Only nobody wanted Joe this morning.

"Wendy? Are you down there?" It was her mother, sounding as though she was talking into a tin can. "You come upstairs this minute and eat your breakfast."

Wendy got into the elevator with Mr. Pick. Standing on tiptoe, she reached past him and pressed 24. And all the way upstairs—ignoring sniffy, squishy Mr. Pick, who got off at 14—she thought about the curious events of the past few minutes.

Bears had come to stay at the Heywood.

Real bears.

Nice bears.

One who had—could it really be?—blue eyes. And another who was scared of her!

Why had they come, and where had they come from, and how had they got here into the city?

And whatever in the world were "cheerings"?

Chapter 2

". . . and I want you to stay upstairs until Joe comes on duty. This is a nice neighborhood, but you just never know what kind of creepy character might wander in off the street."

"Aw, Mom!" You'd think Wendy was a baby who didn't know how to take care of herself. "The outside doors are locked until Joe gets here. Nobody can get in without a key. Only I can open them from the inside, and I wouldn't let . . ."

The words died as Wendy remembered she had opened the doors to strangers that very morning. Hurriedly she took a long sweet swallow of her orange juice, her eyes on the juice, which gave her an interestingly cross-eyed look.

"Don't do that!" her mother protested, laughing. She reached across the table and lifted Wendy's glasses from her face. "Honestly, how do you manage to twist these frames?"

Incredible! This very morning, not fifteen minutes ago, Wendy had been talking to two bears. The world should be all turned around. But here she was in the same old kitchen eating the same old breakfast and being scolded for the same dreary old things she always got scolded for.

Her mother bent one of the bows and handed the glasses back to her. "Try to be a little more careful. They don't grow on a glasses tree, you know."

Wendy licked the last bits of orange from around the rim of her glass and picked up the spoon beside her bowl. She looked at it as if she had never seen a spoon before. "This is a small spoon," she said accusingly. "I never eat my cereal with a small spoon. I always eat it with a big one."

A smile tugged at her mother's mouth.

Wendy looked at her suspiciously. "What's funny?"

"Oh, nothing, really." Her mother dropped bread into the toaster. "It's just that you're so set in your ways."

Wendy got up to find a spoon.

"You know," her mother said thoughtfully, "it wouldn't be a bad idea for you to start setting the table. Then you wouldn't get the wrong kind of spoon. You're not too young for a little responsibility, and—"

CLANG-ANNNG-ANNNG-angangang . . .

It came from upstairs, the sound of something being dropped in the kitchen and rolling round and round for long moments before it stopped with a final, tinny *ank.*

Her mother lifted her eyes to the ceiling. "I thought

12

Dr. what's-his-name was away."

"Corrigan." Wendy supplied the name. Then before her mother could think further about who might be making all that racket upstairs—or, equally bad, get back to "responsibilities"—she said firmly, "I don't like that Mr. Quirk. Why'd you let him eat dinner with us last night, anyway?"

Her mother wrapped her hands around her coffee cup and looked down into it for a moment. Then, "Because he treats me to dinner so often and I guess I just think it's nice to treat him to dinner too." She looked up at Wendy. "Peter likes you, you know."

Wendy shook her head. "Doesn't. He smiled, but he sure didn't want me around." She added darkly, "I could tell."

Her mother was not moved. "Oh, I think you're mistaken, dar—"

CLICK-CLICKETY-CLICK-CLICK-CLICK . . .

The sound was like marbles falling.

Her mother glanced up. "I haven't heard a sound from up there in weeks."

Wendy squirmed. "Maybe Hans or Felix are fixing the sink or something." She turned the conversation back to Mr. Quirk. "Well, he's not as nice as Daddy."

Quiet moved into the kitchen. In the silence the toaster rattled and the toast bounced to the top.

Shadows darkened her mother's eyes. "No, he isn't, Tippy," she said, using the old pet name Wendy had outgrown eons ago. "But then, Daddy cast a long shadow. It's unrealistic to think anyone can measure up to him. I suppose I'll never meet anyone like him again."

"What's that mean, cast a long shadow?"

"Well, Daddy was so—" Her mother chose words carefully, remembering. She seemed to have retreated to a faraway place where Wendy could not follow. "—so intelligent . . . and such fun to be with . . . that his shadow—his memory—extinguishes everyone else's light."

"Well, how can you ask Mr. Ugh to eat dinner with us, then?" Wendy demanded passionately. "I mean, he wears go-along socks."

Her mother looked bewildered. "What?"

Wendy attacked her scrambled eggs. "They always go along with his tie. You know, purple tie, purple socks. Blue tie, blue socks. Last night he even had on go-along shoes!"

"Now, Wendy! You know Peter Quirk has never worn purple anything," protested her mother.

Her mother just did not understand. "Well, if he did wear a purple tie, his socks would be purple too," said Wendy. She expanded on the foibles of Mr. Quirk. "He's so proper. It's like he always folds his napkin, just so. And he pats his mouth, just so. And he wears this eyeball on his tie, this little bitty eyeball, just because he makes eyeglasses. And he doesn't even know that's funny!"

Exasperation and amusement mingled on her mother's face. Amusement won. Laughing, her head back and her mouth open showing her even white teeth, she was the prettiest mother of any Wendy knew.

"He does every one of those things, doesn't he!" She touched her eyes delicately, wiping away tears without smearing her makeup.

"So why?" demanded Wendy.

Her mother sipped her coffee before answering. "Darling, there are two things you'd better know about people. First, you can't tell about them by their clothes. That's only a clue and not the most important one. And second, grown-ups need friends, too, just the way you—"

BANG! CRASH! SCRAAAAPE . . .

Wendy winced. What in heck was going on upstairs? She would give anything if the ceiling were made of see-through wood.

Her mother shuddered. "Tell your friend Dr. Corrigan welcome home. And ask him to be a little quieter." Her eyes lifted to the clock behind Wendy. "Oh, Lord, I'm late for work. Darling, we'll finish this conversation tonight. Now, put your dishes in the sink. And I want you to straighten up your room before you leave for school. I cannot stand looking in there anymore."

On her way out of the kitchen she looked back. "On second thought, don't tell Dr. Corrigan anything. I believe I've told you you're not to bother him. He must be a very busy man."

Wendy gathered up her dishes and set them in the sink with a clatter.

"I said put them in the sink. I didn't say break them," came the clear call from the front of the apartment.

"Do this. Don't do that. Clean up your room. Stay out of the lobby. Don't talk to neat people like Dr. Corrigan," Wendy grumped as she went to her room. It was getting so a person couldn't do anything around here.

She stood in the doorway, wondering where to begin. With its blue walls and white furniture, the room was really very pretty. It was also very messy.

Her mother paused in the hall behind her. "Really, Wendy, this is a pigsty."

Wendy grinned. Her mother had walked right into it. "Pigs are clean. Miss Bunchley said that when we did our farm unit. So you're saying my room is clean."

Her mother wasn't put off. "I'm speaking in the classical sense. Now, no nonsense." She pointed to a half-finished jigsaw puzzle on the floor in one corner. "That's been there for weeks."

16

"Haven't finished it," Wendy explained reasonably.

"Finish." Her mother was hardhearted. "Or put it away. And take those bowls and that sack of plaster out to the kitchen."

The bowls were clustered around a relief map of the United States. "But I've still got to make the Rocky Mountains," Wendy protested. "I need the bowls and stuff." It was really a pretty good map, and it was going to be even better when she painted the rivers and mountains and lakes.

Her mother nodded knowingly. "And you need the magazines on the floor, and you need that pile of shoes, and you need those tights dangling out of the dresser. When I get home this afternoon I want to see this room looking the way it did the day we finished decorating."

She looked at her watch. "Now you've got lunch money, and don't forget your key. Come straight home after school and check in with Mrs. Tulippe. You can go to Kelly's or Sara's, but tell Mrs. Tee if you do. Be home by—"

"Mother," Wendy groaned. "I'm not an infant."

Her mother laughed. "I keep forgetting. I've got a meeting that may run a little late this afternoon." She gave Wendy a quick hug—"Bye, darling!"—and was gone.

Closet doors don't tell secrets about the armloads of shoes and shirts and jeans dumped behind them. Dresser drawers never mention the bunched-up tights and underpants jammed inside. Dust ruffles on beds are the most reliable of all. Not one has ever been known to mention books and magazines safely out of sight behind its pleats. Or almost finished relief maps. Or bowls and plaster.

Hastily Wendy tugged the blankets into place on the bed and covered them with the blue-sprigged coverlet. A denim hat rode the lampshade next to the bed. She transferred it to her head.

There. She stood back, looking around.

Her eyes lit on the puzzle. What was she going to do about that? She sure wasn't going to take it apart —it was one of the hard kind with a picture on both sides. Maybe her mother wouldn't notice it if the rest of her stuff was put away. She dragged a chair across the room and placed it kitty-corner in front of the puzzle.

There wasn't a single thing her mother could complain about this afternoon—if she didn't open the closet or the dresser drawers or look under the bed.

The day was endless. She couldn't keep her mind on things like fractions and the Mississippi, nor even on making batik in Indonesia. Not when she thought about the morning. She was practically bouncing in her seat when the bell finally rang. She dashed for her locker.

"We're going to my house," called Kelly.

"I'm bringing my new Danny McCracken record," added Sara.

"My mother bought napoleons for her club," said Kelly, smacking her lips. "There'll be some for us."

"Can't come." Wendy thrust her arms into her jacket, nearly hitting Sara. "I promised to go straight home." No excuses. No explanations.

Kelly looked surprised but didn't protest. "Well, okay." Her eyes lit. "That means Sara and I can have more napoleons. If my mother will let us."

Wendy ran all the way to the Heywood. She dropped her books in the apartment, then knocked on Mrs. Tulippe's door to tell her she was home.

Inside, the door chain rattled and locks turned. Distracted words filtered through the door. "Dear, dear. Oh, mercy."

Mrs. Tulippe believed in being safe. Besides the chain, she had four kinds of slides and bolts, and it always took a while to get them in the unlocked position all at the same time. Someday Mrs. Tulippe wouldn't be able to figure them out and would be locked inside forevermore.

The door opened at last and a very old lady beamed down at Wendy. Her hair was faintly blue, and she wore rhinestone earrings and tottery high-heeled shoes. She took her duties to Wendy seriously.

"Now you just come in, dear. Tell me all about school." She closed the door and bolted all the locks.

"And have some cookies. And have some milk."

Wendy was going to explode right out of her skin if she had to stay around and talk to Mrs. Tulippe. She followed the old lady to the kitchen. "I don't want any milk today. I'm going out." She eyed the cookies on a plate on the table. Gingersnaps. The best kind Mrs. Tulippe made. The bears might like them too. "But I sure would like to take my cookies with me. Uh—I bet—uh—Kelly and Sara would love some gingersnaps too," she hinted.

"You'll want more, then," Mrs. Tulippe said helpfully, and while she put them in a paper bag, Wendy had to make her promises. No, she wouldn't talk to strangers in the park. Yes, she would be indoors by five.

With enormous relief she got away from Mrs. Tulippe and heard the locks fall into place behind her.

Elevators were too slow. She let herself into the stairwell and ran upstairs.

Her hand on the shiny brass knocker of 2502, she shivered slightly, then let the knocker fall. The hollow thud sounded like thunder in the silent hall. With a forefinger she pushed at the bridge of her glasses and waited to see what she would find on the other side of the door.

Chapter 3

With only the faintest click of the lock, the door opened a narrow slit. Nobody was to be seen.

"Who's that?" came a rumbling whisper.

"It's me." Wendy kept her voice low, glancing over her shoulder. "Wendy."

The door swung inward. "Come in, child."

Quickly, before someone came into the hall from one of the other apartments, she slipped inside and the door closed. The bear standing behind it smiled at her.

Gone were the outlandish clothes. Otto was revealed simply as a bear, a softly furry bear. Comfortably round, not much taller than Wendy, he was quite the handsomest bear she had ever seen. His fur was the old gold of sand in the early morning sun, except for the tips of his ears and nose and paws, which were a deep seal brown. His mouth was a happy one—mouths only get that way from smiling a lot—and a smile played, too, in the depths of the astonishing blue eyes.

Wendy, clutching her bag of gingersnaps, found

herself smiling back. Apparently looking at Otto made you do that. "I came as soon as I could," she said.

Something moved in the shadowy hall that led from the foyer to the living room and den and beyond.

Lifting his voice slightly, Otto spoke into the shadows. "It came to see us, love. Just as it said it would. I do think it's all right."

Ursula Ma'am had to be the shyest creature in the whole world. Wendy had always thought Sara got the blue ribbon for shyness. Sara was so shy she threw up on the first day of school every single year. It had taken Miss Bunchley a month to get her to say even one word in class. But there had to be a super blue ribbon for Ursula Ma'am. She was so shy it seemed she wanted to be invisible.

Wendy spoke toward the hall, keeping her voice soft. "I gave my word. I won't tell." It was the best you could do, give your word. "I wouldn't hurt you. Not for anything."

She remembered the gingersnaps. "Mrs. Tulippe makes the best cookies. They're my after-school snack. You can have Kelly's and Sara's."

"Something to eat!" Beside her, Otto beamed. "Did you hear that, love?"

The shadows stirred and Ursula Ma'am emerged. She smiled warily, her voice the merest whisper. "Hello, child."

She was only slightly smaller than Otto, and her

coloring matched his. Her mouth, too, turned upward at the corners. Her eyes, blue as his, held a promise of laughter—and a puzzling something Wendy could find no name for. And the way she stood—tall somehow, in spite of her smallness—said even more. Ursula Ma'am was in some important way different from Otto.

Wendy realized she was staring and offered the gingersnaps.

As one, the bears reached into the bag, bumping paws in their eagerness. Otto bit into his, swallowed, smacked his lips, and ate the rest in a single gulp. Ursula Ma'am's disappeared almost as rapidly.

Wendy offered the cookies again. "You're pretty hungry, I guess."

An idea prodded Ursula Ma'am out of her silence. "Otto dear, it must know about the—the—" She searched for a word, gave up, gestured vaguely toward the back of the apartment.

Otto stopped in mid-bite. "The opener thing!" He explained to Wendy. "There is food there." Again the vague wave. "But it's all shut up in hard things. There is an opener thing to get the food out, but we cannot make it work. If you—"

"Oh my gosh!" Suddenly Wendy understood. "Didn't you get to eat anything all day?"

The bleakness in their eyes gave her the answer.

"You must be hollow! Come on!"

The pine-paneled kitchen was at the other end of the book-lined hall, just as it was downstairs, and Wendy led the way. On the counter were cans of fruit and apple juice and a can opener. A green ring binder lay beside them, opened to a page that showed drawings of different kinds of cans and a can opener.

Wendy remembered the racket at breakfast. "You sure did a lot of banging around up here this morning."

"We were looking for the food." Otto opened a low cupboard next to the stove and touched a pan cover. "This fell out. And then I dropped some of the cheerings—"

That word again. That peculiar word. *Cheerings.*

He pointed to the step stool. "And I pushed that thing to climb on it, and it fell over."

"And after all that, you found the food and then you couldn't open the cans!" Wendy couldn't imagine being hungry for a whole day. She would have perished.

She picked up the can opener. "Hey, look. This is easy." Deftly she sliced around the top of a can of pears. The bears watched, deeply interested.

"And juice you open with a"—she searched through the cutlery drawer—"can poker!" She held it up triumphantly and then punched two neat holes in the top of the juice can. She spooned fruit into bowls and poured the golden juice into mugs. "There."

They ate ravenously. When they had finished, they went to the sink and rinsed the bowls and spoons. Standing on tiptoe, they put them back in the cupboard, wet but clean.

Otto smiled at her astonishment. "Dr. Corrigan said to do that," he explained. He dropped the pear can into the wastebasket under the sink. "He said if humans come in here and see eating things, they will know someone is here."

It all made sense. Only, who would come into Dr. Corrigan's apartment? And if people did, wouldn't they see Otto and Ursula Ma'am? So what difference did it make about dishes?

It was all too much to think about . . .

Dr. Corrigan's living room was an inviting place of brightness and books. Tall windows looked northward, out over the city, with a clear view of the lake to the east. Bookshelves lined the walls. Books overflowed the shelves onto the floor. They were piled on the windowsills. They rested in uneasy towers on the tables. Even the comfortable big chairs sagged under the weight of books.

Making room on the coffee table for the cookies, Wendy pushed aside more books . . . a tennis racket . . . a guitar. The table was revealed as an expanse of greenish glass supported by an immense bark-covered tree stump. There was a gasp behind her.

"From the mountain," breathed Ursula Ma'am,

clasping her paws in delight. Her eyes sparkled, her fears forgotten for the moment.

With a lopsided grin, Otto settled on the floor. He reached under the table and scratched at the bark. "All the way from the mountain!"

Wendy looked at the bears in astonishment. Imagine getting all that overheated about a slice of tree!

She sank cross-legged onto the thick carpeting, leaned an elbow on the table, prodded her glasses with a forefinger, and asked the thing she had been wondering about. "What are cheerings?"

A shadow returned to Ursula Ma'am's eyes. "They are the—the—good earth things we brought to"—her velvety voice became even softer—"to cheer us while we wait, and later . . ." The sentence dangled.

The room was still except for muted sounds that rose from Sheridan Road. The quiet thunder of endlessly passing traffic. The sullen grumble of a bus starting up at the corner.

Otto cleared his throat. "Well, I'll show you."

He padded out of the room and returned with the hump-shaped valise. Reaching in with cupped paws, he lifted them over the table and spilled pebbles onto the polished surface. More pebbles and larger stones of different colors and shapes followed.

Wendy stared in disbelief. Stones? The cheerings were only stones! Whatever she had been expecting, it had not been stones!

26

Ursula Ma'am leaned forward. She picked up a piece of pink quartz, admiring it as she might have admired a priceless jewel. Wendy seemed forgotten.

Otto lifted a translucent piece to the light, revealing deep-toned swirls of amber and orange in its center. "Like the sunset," he said, almost to himself. Then, to Wendy, "Found it. In a cave. No human ever walked there. No human ever saw this." He laid it in Wendy's palm. "Only you have, now." And it was as though he placed an honor and a trust upon her.

Suddenly awed, Wendy turned the stone. This stone might have lain in that cave since the world began. And now she was touching it. The very first person.

She held it to the light. It was truly beautiful. She hadn't known stones could be beautiful. Stones were what you fell down and scraped your knees on. And that had been her only thought about stones—if she had ever considered them at all.

She replaced the stone on the table.

And she still did not understand. The stones seemed to mean something more than just beauty to the bears. "To cheer us," Ursula Ma'am had said, "while we wait," and "later."

Wendy pulled her blond braid over her shoulder, played with the end, and looked from Otto to Ursula Ma'am. "But what does it all mean?" she demanded.

Otto swept the pebbles into a pile before answering. And then he didn't really reply to Wendy's question. "We are being hunted, child. By humans."

Wendy's let-out breath sounded like air escaping from a balloon. "But why? Did you steal something? Or—or—" Or what? What laws could bears break?

"We are bears. That's all." Ursula Ma'am said the words. Gone was the contentment of a moment ago. "Bears."

"Ther-r-re ar-r-re not many like us." Otto's voice was low and tense, his *r*'s heavy. "The humans want to save us."

"That means they want to put us on a little"— Ursula Ma'am held her paws narrowly together— "land."

"Har-r-rdly big enough for a mountain or two," growled Otto.

"And around it they will put a—a—" Ursula Ma'am stumbled over the word.

"A fence, Dr-r-r. Cor-r-rigan called it," said Otto.

"Yes, a fence. And if we walk toward the morning sun, or the evening sun, we will meet that fence." Ursula Ma'am's voice quivered. "And if at night we walk toward the glow star, we will come to that fence. And if . . ." There was no need to continue.

Wendy's mind was whirling. What Ursula Ma'am was saying sounded as bad as being in jail.

"Dr-r-r. Cor-r-rigan says the humans mean well. But they don't know a bear-r-r has got to be"—Otto came down hard on the word—"FR-R-REE."

"They don't know," said Ursula Ma'am, "that even if the land is so big it takes many sunrises to walk over it, if at the edge you cannot go on to the next mountain, that is a wicked thing."

A chill touched Wendy. It all sounded so desperate. Otto and Ursula Ma'am couldn't stay on their mountain. But neither could they stay in Dr. Corrigan's apartment forever. Or, at least she didn't think they could.

"What are you going to do?" The question burst from her.

Otto watched her intently. "Already did something." He was calmer. "Do you know about the big dipper, child?"

Didn't Otto ever give a straight answer to a straight question? Wendy answered, nevertheless. "Do you mean the stars?"

He gave a single brisk nod.

"You can't see them much in the city," Wendy explained. "The lights are too bright. But I saw the big dipper last summer when I visited my grandpa in Michigan. It was really dark there." She remembered. She had been afraid of the inky blackness of the night, and the utter stillness of the country. Grandpa had taken her hand.

"Did you know the big dipper used to be called the Great Bear?" asked Otto. "Us bears still call it that."

"It has another name too," Ursula Ma'am added

softly. "Ursa Major. Ursa—that means bear."

"Do you know about legends?" It was Otto again. Wendy felt as though she was being led on a game of leapfrog, blindfolded, in a place she had never been before. But she did her best to keep up. "Like Pluto, and Persephone, and the Underworld?"

"We don't know about them, exactly," said Ursula Ma'am. "But we know humans have legends. And us bears have ours too. Our legends say the Great Bear wasn't called that for nothing."

"There are bears there," Otto said proudly. "On a little world near one of the stars in the dipper. It has a name. It's called Brūn."

"We sent them a message," Ursula Ma'am said matter-of-factly.

"But how!" This was the most incredible tale Wendy had ever heard.

"Dr. Corrigan," said Otto. "Before the snows came, he gave us a talk thing."

"All winter we sent messages on the talk thing," said Ursula Ma'am.

"The bears, the Others, heard us," Otto added calmly. "They sent a message back. They are coming here to get us."

"Here?" Wendy blurted.

"Here," rumbled Otto, laughing at her astonishment.

Ursula Ma'am took a deep breath. "Right here."

30

Chapter 4

"Dr. Corrigan listened to us about our legends. Then one day he brought the talk thing. 'Try to send a message to those Others,' he said. And so we did."

They were in Dr. Corrigan's kitchen, and Otto bit into his very first toasted peanut-butter-and-jelly sandwich. He licked his lips.

Her eyes on the sandwich Wendy was putting together, Ursula Ma'am said, "Every day we sent messages. We sent them the bear way, so humans couldn't understand."

She took the warm nutty-smelling sandwich Wendy offered and nibbled. Her lips turned up at the corners.

Wendy slid into a chair and flipped her braid forward over her shoulder. She fingered it, waiting for more of the bears' story.

It was the next morning, Saturday. Getting away from her mother had not been easy.

Mrs. Devlin had to go to the office to check some sketches so the artist could pick them up that afternoon. It was a rush job.

As she brushed her hair, she worried about going

away on a day when Wendy was home from school. "We'll make it up," she assured her. "On my next free Saturday—whenever that is—we'll go to the pool. Or the Museum of Science and Industry."

Wendy was picking out jewelry to go with her mother's outfit. She slid a ring onto her thumb and turned it, admiring the shift of colors in the opal. "I don't mind being alone. And anyway, I don't have to be alone if I don't want to. Kelly and Sara were talking about going to the Planetarium."

So then her mother supposed Wendy was going to the Planetarium, too, and of course she worried—she worried more efficiently than anyone Wendy knew— about eating properly—

"No junk food," W   mised.

—and about talking to strangers—

That was so dumb Wendy didn't look up from the velvet-lined jewel case. Who would talk to strangers?

—and about getting on the right bus—

"Aw, Mom," Wendy groaned. "I've been getting on the right bus since I was seven."

Her mother laughed. She took the antique bracelet Wendy offered and fastened the clip. "I keep forgetting how big you're getting."

Thoughtful, Wendy studied the opal. It was a stone. Maybe— "Does this stone cheer you up?" she asked.

Her mother looked startled. "What a funny way to put it. That belonged to Great-aunt Maggie. And yes,

I suppose it does cheer me. I think of her when I wear it. Only I'm not about to, with this pants outfit. That's a dinner ring."

Wendy put it back in the velvet tray. The opal was a precious stone. The cheerings were in some way precious too. Only not like the opal.

She had watched through the half-open door and waved when her mother stepped into the elevator. Then, remembering yesterday, and the forlorn look of hunger in Otto and Ursula Ma'am's eyes, she had gone to the kitchen and gathered up anything there was a lot of—bread, an extra jar of peanut butter, jelly, apples—and let herself out into the back hall.

She had come up the service stairway, the soft slapping of her bare feet on the cement steps and the rustle of the food in the paper sack echoing hollowly in the bleakly lit gray cavern. And here she was, sitting in Dr. Corrigan's sunny kitchen.

Three opened cans were lined up on the sink. She squinted, trying to see the labels. "What'd you have for breakfast?"

"Peaches." Otto spoke around his sandwich. "And plums. Not as good as the tree kind, but tasty."

Ursula Ma'am laughed in her engagingly breathy way. "We had a surprise too." She pointed.

The third can had no picture. Wendy went to look. It was nearly full of black olives. "Fancy imported extra large black olives," she read from the label.

33

"Ugh. I detest the black kind. They're for parties."

Otto and Ursula Ma'am exchanged knowing glances. What else could be expected of humans?

"A most curious custom," rumbled Otto.

Ursula Ma'am finished the thought. "To eat things you do not like at parties."

"Grown-up parties," Wendy explained. "Grown-ups like the queerest things, like clams and anchovies and"—she made a face—"cream cheese. I really detest cream cheese."

She emptied the can into the garbage disposal, turned on the water, and flicked the switch. The gurgling clatter brought the bears to watch, their eyes enormous. Wendy let the disposal run until there was only the sound of sloshing water.

When the kitchen was still again, Ursula Ma'am was the first to speak. "What is *that?*" She looked terrified.

Wendy explained. "Only you're not supposed to put cans in it," she said, dropping the empty cans into the waste basket under the sink.

Otto was slightly pale. It showed around his nose. "You can't get anything back from down there?"

"It just chops everything up and washes it away," Wendy said breezily.

"Don't like it," Ursula Ma'am said with finality. She shuddered. "It's an awful gone-forever thing."

Returning to the polished pine table, Otto said

firmly, "We won't do that anymore."

He swallowed the last of his sandwich and cheered up. "Humans have got some good things, though." He brushed the crumbs from the table into his paw, tipped up his chin, and dropped them into his mouth. "Like this food."

Wendy grinned. "My most favorite kind of sandwiches." She sobered. "But look. If you don't like the garbage disposal because it takes things away forever, how do you feel about going away from the earth, maybe forever?"

The question hung in the air.

Otto cleared his throat. "Can't let the humans put that fence around us."

Ursula Ma'am, her eyes glistening, looked straight into Wendy's eyes. "We must be free." She took a trembling breath. "So we will trade our beautiful mountain for whatever"—she gave a helpless little shrug—"is there."

Wendy couldn't imagine what it would be like to go away from the earth. From her mother and Sara and Kelly and the Heywood and Jasper Quentin Osgood School. Never to see the lake again, or the museum.

That other planet. Did it have mountains and trees? All she could think of was the barren surface of the moon. She was sure she wouldn't want to live on the moon.

Ursula Ma'am continued. "We have cheerings to

look at, and cheerings to touch. You saw some of those. And we have cheerings to plant." Her voice grew stronger. "We will make that place, that Brūn, beautiful, if it is not."

Questions bubbled in Wendy's mind, too many questions to ask all at once. She settled for getting started on the first. "I guess a 'talk thing' is a radio."

Otto and Ursula Ma'am looked at her, not understanding.

"Well, I mean, do you talk into it and does it carry your voice far away? And does it bring other voices to you?"

Otto shook his head vigorously. No. "Music."

Ursula Ma'am explained. "We play bear music. Bear music comes back."

That was close enough. "That's a radio," Wendy decided. "Well, then, how did you send messages that everyone didn't understand? I mean, people?"

Otto and Ursula Ma'am exchanged a look. Should they tell this little human a most privileged secret? Ursula Ma'am looked at her quietly for a moment, then nodded her approval.

"Humans cannot understand the message in our music," said Otto.

"It is hidden," explained Ursula Ma'am. "In the highs and the lows. In the swiftness and the slowness of it. In the melody. Only bears understand it."

"You mean you *talk* in music?"

36

Otto frowned. "Well, not talk."

Ursula Ma'am said in final explanation, "It's just there. We understand."

Mr. Gautier, Wendy's French teacher, had said something like that one day about French. "I just understand." Bear music—to bears—must be like that.

"Hardly got a good week's sleep all winter, waking up to send messages," said Otto.

A tender look passed over Ursula Ma'am's face. "The snow melted after a while. The flowers came, and the high warmth. Dr. Corrigan came back to the mountain. And after that we heard faraway music on the talk thing. Bear music, it was." She smiled, remembering. "The most beautiful music."

"But then," Otto's voice roughened, "Dr-r-r. Cor-r-ri-gan found out about the humans looking for-r-r us."

Ursula Ma'am clasped and unclasped her paws. "He said we must go away from the mountain to a place where those humans would not look for us while we waited for the Others."

"Dr-r-r. Cor-r-rigan, he said we would be safe here." Otto pointed at the green ring binder. "Made us pictures of things to know. Brought us the fur hiders."

Fur hiders? He had to mean the coats and hats, Wendy decided.

"His friend brought us to the city in a flying thing."

Ursula Ma'am's eyes were enormous. "We were like a bird."

"He gave something to the human in the yellow—yellow—"

"Car." Wendy supplied the word. "Taxi."

"Thing," said Otto. "And he told him to bring us here. And he did."

"But didn't the taxi driver look at you?" asked Wendy. "Didn't he try to talk to you?"

Otto shook his head. "He kept doing this." He yawned behind a lifted paw. "I think he was sleepy."

"It was all very easy," Ursula Ma'am said innocently.

Easy! If it had seemed easy, surely it was only because Dr. Corrigan had made it seem so. There had to be more to this story, and someday Wendy would pry it out of him.

"Yes, but how could you—"

Her question was cut off by the rattle and clank of machinery sounding from the hall. The ancient service elevator was moving in its shaft.

Their eyes riveted to the kitchen door, they waited, breath held, as the noise grew louder. With a solid metallic clank, the elevator stopped and the doors clanged open.

The back of Wendy's neck prickled.

Men's voices sounded in the hall.

"Quick!" she whispered, touching her lips. She sprinted out of the kitchen, down the hall, into the den.

Otto and Ursula Ma'am sped after her on their soft, padded bears' feet. As they entered the den, a key turning in the kitchen door echoed through the silent apartment.

Alert, Wendy scanned the room. The long closet on the west wall—it would be shallow, like the one in her bedroom below.

A deep voice came from the kitchen. It was Hans, the engineer. ". . . check out the garbage disposal. I'll look at the fan. She can't 've heard anything, though. Corrigan's not here."

The words carried into the den with terrifying clarity.

Desperately Wendy looked around. The door in the far corner had to lead into a deep storage closet. Pushing down panic, she darted across the room and eased the door open. The soft squeak of its hinges was like a scream in the quiet room.

The talk went on in the kitchen.

"Hey, boss. There's water in the sink." That was Felix, Hans's helper.

". . . wore-out washer. Say, do you smell bread toasting?"

Otto and Ursula Ma'am were rooted at the door, looking scared, glancing from Wendy to the hall behind them.

"Come on," Wendy whispered hoarsely. In the breath of time it took to shepherd them into the closet,

39

she was aware of immense clutter. Then she slid the door shut.

Ribbons of light came through the slatted door. In the stuffy twilight they picked their way among skis, ski boots, an Exercycle, golf clubs, nested flower pots, empty picture frames, and stacks of books.

The thud of footsteps moving through the apartment reached into the closet. Behind the clothes at the back, pressed against the wall, Wendy bit her lip. Her mouth was dry, her cheeks hot. In the darkness, a trembling paw took her left hand and another sought her right. She squeezed them comfortingly.

An eternity passed. Then the voices were clear again. The men had come into the den.

"Funny, I never noticed those old suitcases in here before." That was Hans.

Pause. Something was set down with a bang. "That Corrigan's sure got a place full of wild stuff," said Felix.

The doors of the closet across the room clattered open and after a long moment rattled shut.

Footsteps crossed the room.

Wendy shivered. Beside her, Otto muffled a soft hiccup. Ursula Ma'am clutched her hand until it hurt.

"Don't move," Wendy breathed. "Shut your eyes."

The door of the storage closet opened.

Chapter 5

Hands clutched, Wendy and the bears huddled behind the jackets and coats at the back of the closet,
rigid, wanting to see what was happening, yet not
daring to open their eyes.

Fumblety-clump. The golf clubs rattled.

Thump-slide. Skis moved against the wall.

Grate-clank. Flowerpots jiggled.

When would searching hands come pushing through
the clothes? A dew of perspiration broke out on
Wendy's forehead.

Splack-splack-splack! A stack of books tumbled to
the floor.

"Messy closet," muttered Felix. There was the slapping sound of the books being restacked.

A pedal of the Exercycle whirred into noisy motion. It stopped. There was a long silence.

What was Felix doing?

Pause.

"Hey, boss?"

Pause.

Footsteps approached.

"Look at this."

Look at what? A shudder passed from Ursula Ma'am to Wendy and on to Otto.

Pause.

"Never saw so much stuff crammed into one place in my life. Think we gotta search it?"

Pause.

Hans's reply was firm. "Nah. Can't be anyone in there. Come on. Let's go."

The closet door clacked shut.

Wendy and the bears sagged against each other in relief. She dared, then, to open her eyes. Pushing aside a down ski parka and a corduroy jacket, she picked her way through the clutter and put her ear to the door.

The men's voices came from the kitchen again.

". . . wore-out washer . . . faucet . . . fix next week . . ."

"Old lady . . . imagined she heard . . . here."

There was more that couldn't be made out, followed by the slamming of the kitchen door.

With a heady feeling of relief, Wendy stepped out into the den, blinking in the sunlight. She tiptoed to the hall door and listened.

The apartment was so quiet she heard a birdsong from somewhere outside. The place felt empty. She moved into the hall, peered into the living room, inspected the dining room. Advancing toward the kitchen, her feet dragged. Just because the door had slammed, it didn't mean Hans and Felix were really on the other side of it. It could all be a trap! Maybe they were still in the kitchen, waiting for some bad guy to appear. Maybe . . .

The service elevator groaned to a start, erasing her fears. Relieved, she peeked into the kitchen. It was deserted.

"Come on out," she whispered jubilantly, racing back to the den. "They're gone."

Otto and Ursula Ma'am emerged from the back of the closet, high-stepping over books and ski boots.

Otto shook himself as though to rid himself of the fear of the last minutes. It was a lighthearted movement, but his words were not in the least lighthearted. "A human could come and catch us her-r-re. Easy."

It was true. "They're coming back to fix something in the sink," Wendy admitted. "I don't know when."

Ursula Ma'am's eyes lifted upward almost as though she expected to see someone staring down from the ceiling. "There's a terrible human up there who hears things." She looked miserable. "I think we cannot even talk."

"That's Mrs. Constable. She's really old and she never goes out," Wendy explained, adding comfortingly, "She can't hear us talking. It's only the big noises like the garbage disposal that she can hear. I think."

Otto brightened. "And we aren't going to do that anymore." There would be nothing more to hear. So much for the terrible human upstairs.

His glance fell on the roped suitcases he had carried so carefully yesterday morning. His cheer increased. Here was something a bear in a bad corner could *do*. "Got messages to send," he rumbled, and hunkered down before the suitcases.

The knots were frayed tangles. "All we've got to do is get them open. Tried and tried yesterday."

Wendy knelt. "I'm a pretty good unknotter. I learned in Brownies."

She worked at the rope. Her forehead puckered. The knots were hopeless, even for a skilled unknotter.

A chef would have winced at the use to which Wendy put the fine German steel knife she found in a rack in the kitchen. Fortunately, none was around to see. She sawed at the prickly rope and the strands began to separate with satisfying little popping sounds. The rope snapped apart and she looked up.

Otto and Ursula Ma'am's eyes were locked. Finally Ursula Ma'am spoke. "It didn't tell."

Otto nodded. "I knew it was a nice one. It is a brave little one as well."

They were talking about her again!

"If the humans found us, they would have found it too." Ursula Ma'am shuddered. "Who knows what terrible thing they would have done?"

Her eyes dropped to Wendy's. The look was open and trusting. Her lips curved in a sunny smile. "Thank you, child."

If Wendy hadn't been on her knees, she would have bobbed another curtsey. As it was, she grinned and pushed her glasses back into place. "I like helping you," she said simply.

Happily she started on the second suitcase. Both were at last opened to reveal the two parts of a kind of radio.

Otto stroked them. "Our talk thing," he said quietly, as though addressing an old friend. He busied himself matching wires of various colors and joining them. From time to time he compared the wires to those in a drawing in the green ring binder.

Wendy recognized the bold pencil strokes and clear, pictured directions. It was like one of the drawings Dr. Corrigan sometimes made for her down at the museum, to show her how a prehistoric skeleton looked when it was discovered embedded in a cliff.

Ursula Ma'am was searching the depths of the valise. After much rattling about, she withdrew a flutelike instrument and came to sit on the floor next to Otto.

The flute was like none Wendy had ever seen. Neither perfectly straight nor perfectly round, it showed clearly the shape of the small branch from which it had been made. It had been stripped of its bark but had remained green, the pale green of the first feathering leaves of springtime. Ursula Ma'am held it delicately, positioning her paws over the openings.

Otto unwound an electrical cord. "Never needed this on the mountain. Dr. Corrigan said to fasten it to the wall here, though."

"I'll do it," Wendy offered. She strung the cord across the room and plugged it into an outlet.

Otto examined the control panel, seemed satisfied, then turned to Ursula Ma'am. She lifted the instrument to her lips, nodded her readiness, and he touched the switch.

Static exploded into the room. It bounced off the walls, quivered in the air. Wendy's very bones vibrated with it.

The three sat stunned, unmoving in the instant— the eternity—before Otto came to life and flipped the switch. The red light on the panel paled and died, and with it the bombardment of grating noise.

In the street far below a siren approached, grew loud, faded as it passed.

"That's not what it's supposed to do," Ursula Ma'am whispered.

Otto reached out to the radio, then hesitated as though fearful the "talk thing" would come alive again of its own will. "Something's most ter-r-rible wr-r-rong!" His *r*'s clearly reflected his concern.

Wendy voiced the fearful question. "If you can't use the radio, how will those other bears know where to find you?"

Neither Otto nor Ursula Ma'am replied. They looked at her, mutely acknowledging the certain truth: Without the radio, there was no way for the Others to find the Heywood.

Ursula Ma'am was the first to remember the more immediate danger. "The humans! They will come back to look for this new noise."

In frantic haste they disconnected the colored wires, unplugged the radio, and returned it to the suitcases. Otto strapped them shut, and they waited in a huddle of misery for the sound of a key in the kitchen door.

Otto had the hiccups again. The silence was punctuated by the abrupt little sounds. Ursula Ma'am had lifted an extraordinarily large pine cone—bigger than Wendy's arm—from the valise. She cradled it lovingly, rocking gently. She seemed to have shut out Otto, Wendy, the Heywood, the city.

The minutes on the digital clock on the desk flipped past. Five minutes. Ten minutes.

Wendy began to feel easier. "Do you know what I think? I think if Mrs. Constable called the office again and said she heard noises, they didn't believe her."

More minutes passed. For whatever reason, the men

did not return. With growing confidence, Wendy said, "I'll bet you don't have to worry until Monday, either. Because Felix goes home at noon on Saturday and Hans won't come on weekends except if it's an emergency."

Slowly their panic dissolved.

They had to test the radio again, just to be sure. Otto reassembled it. With a lightning movement he opened and closed the switch. A needle of sound darted through the room and was instantly extinguished. So that was that.

Otto sat back on his heels, looking at it. "Dr. Corrigan said he would talk to us on the ring thing. He will tell us how to make it well."

The ring thing? Wendy's question showed on her face.

"The thing will ring," Otto explained, "and I am to say hello and Dr. Corrigan will talk—"

"The telephone!" exclaimed Wendy.

"He can tell us how to fix the talk thing," said Ursula Ma'am. "Dr. Corrigan, he knows everything," she finished with the simple faith of innocence.

The rest of that strange and frightening day was like no other Wendy had ever spent.

They ate again. When their stomachs still growled in hunger, she fixed more peanut-butter sandwiches, the food which seemed to lift the bears' spirits. Then she dug about in the canned goods cupboard, searching for fruit.

Otto and Ursula Ma'am looked over her shoulders, identifying the foods in the pictures.

"Apples," murmured Ursula Ma'am, sounding pleased.

"Fish!" exclaimed a delighted Otto, reaching for a can of sardines.

Ursula Ma'am offered a can for Wendy's inspection.

Wendy read the label. "Smoked sliced—octopus?" Her voice slid up in disgust. "In cottonseed oil. Double ugh!" She pushed it to the back of the shelf where the bears wouldn't get it by mistake. "I don't like that and neither would you."

Also to the back went imported herring in tomato sauce, Strasbourg pâté de foie gras, smoked oysters, and other suspicious cans. The things her mother served at parties. Grown-ups really had weird tastes!

Happily, Wendy found things she approved of. At the front of the shelf she arranged cherries, peaches, pears, and other fruit. Behind them went tuna, salmon, canned lunch meat, and hash. There were plenty of dreary-looking vegetables too. She pushed those toward the back, as next-to-last resorts.

She studied the shelf. How much food did two smallish bears need? Was there enough for a week? Two days? Two weeks?

After lunch, in the living room, Ursula Ma'am tumbled cheering stones onto the coffee table. More followed, and still more. Agate. Obsidian. Mica. Jasper. Quartz. Wendy didn't know those names, of course. Only later would she learn them.

Thoughtful, she studied them, wondering again what made them precious. A small piece, pale lavender in color, caught her eye. She placed it on the back of her hand, on her ring finger. "Now I've got a ring," she said, showing it to Otto.

Gently, Otto removed it from her hand. "That's the human way of things. Us bears do things the bear way."

Deftly he pushed the pebbles into a shaded pattern of colors. "Fields of flowers," he said softly, looking closely at Wendy for her reaction.

Wendy stared. She had never seen a mountainside in flower. Yet on the table, in the arrangement of the pebbles, she had—not exactly a glimpse—an impression, rather, of a star-flowered meadow.

She didn't have long to enjoy it. Beside her, Ursula Ma'am laughed softly. With a flick of her paw she rearranged the stones. "This"—she worked in quick, circular motions—"is" . . . a mosaic was forming . . . "stars at night," she finished triumphantly.

A prickle of delight ran through Wendy. There was the big dipper! There seemed to be other constellations too. She had seen them in a book about stars.

Otto, not to be outdone, carried on the game. "Clouds." The patterns shifted. "White"—he worked rapidly—"rabbits in the sky!"

"Rain in sunshine," crowed Ursula Ma'am, and the picture formed.

"Running streams," laughed Otto, not to be outdone.

"Sunset!"

"Sunrise!"

Dazzled, Wendy saw—or sensed—them all. It was better than any word game she had ever played. Better than any puzzle she had ever put together.

Laughing, Otto and Ursula Ma'am rested from their efforts.

Going down the back stairway in time to meet her mother at two o'clock, Wendy couldn't get the cheerings out of her head. How was it possible that those things comforted the bears? She knew she wouldn't be comforted by some stones or a pine cone if she had to go away—forever!—from a place she loved as much as Otto and Ursula Ma'am loved their mountain. Not if there was someone chasing her . . . and her radio didn't work . . . and there was no way to get word to those "Others" who were coming to rescue her. *Especially* not if she was stuck in an apartment with nobody to help her. Except her. Wendy.

Chapter 6

Getting back upstairs the next day wasn't easy. It was Sunday and Mr. Quirk took Mrs. Devlin and Wendy to brunch at the Pickle Barrel. Wendy ate a bagel and lox—without any cream cheese, but with lots of sweet, thin-sliced onions. And she had three French doughnuts. She was sliding out of her chair to go back to the buffet for a fourth when Mrs. Devlin, who had been deep in conversation with Mr. Quirk, noticed her. "Wendy! You'll turn into a sausage. You're just at that age!"

"Let her go, Barbara." Mr. Quirk winked at Wendy. "A few doughnuts never hurt us. Right, chum?"

Wendy sank back into her chair, her chin burrowed into her collar. It was remarkable how the hole in her middle suddenly filled. She didn't want another doughnut. She didn't want anything Mr. Ugh thought was okay.

While her mother and Mr. Quirk talked about Mozart, Wendy cracked peanuts from the bowl in the center of the table and slid the nuts into her pockets. Otto and Ursula Ma'am would like them.

What were the bears doing? Were they eating? Had they tried the radio again? And had it worked?

She didn't even get to go home after brunch. Because Mr. Quirk said—with another broad wink at Wendy—that the zoo would be "just swell." And naturally her mother agreed. Wendy could almost see her thinking how great it was that old ugh-face was being nice to her child.

Wendy had always loved the zoo. Today was different, though.

Smashed peanut shells and marshmallows fallen short of the reach of the animals in the cages seemed— Seemed what? With newborn awareness she watched the monkeys begging for peanuts, the coyotes restlessly pacing in their cages. And for the first time she wondered about the bars. Bars that separated the animals from each other. Bars that separated the animals from her.

She searched their dull eyes. Were they happy? Could they talk to her if they wanted to?

None of the animals' eyes met hers. None looked as though it could, or would even want to, talk.

Maybe her good feelings about the zoo would never come back. . . .

"Cat's got someone's tongue," said Mr. Quirk as they climbed onto the bus that would take them home.

Wendy didn't answer. She ran to the back of the bus so she could look out the window there. And think about the animals. And be away from Mr. Ugh.

Her mother had a new Haydn record. Late in the afternoon, while the grown-ups listened to it, Wendy slipped upstairs.

"I brought you a surprise," she said, emptying her pockets on the coffee table. Peanuts bounced and rolled in every direction.

Ursula Ma'am's nose quivered.

Otto's eyes glittered—as they seemed to whenever he saw food of any kind. "I'll try some." He chewed thoughtfully for a minute, then scooped the peanuts into a pile in front of him. He looked very serious. "I better eat these so you don't get sick, love," he said.

"Oh." Ursula Ma'am's head drooped. "And they smelled so—"

Otto's deep chuckle interrupted her. "Just jollying you, love."

Ursula Ma'am's smile returned as she sampled the peanuts.

"Did you try to make the radio work?" asked Wendy.

Two heads nodded a brisk yes.

"Did it?"

The two heads moved back and forth. No. "And Dr. Corrigan did not talk to us on the ring thing, either," added Otto.

Ursula Ma'am's faith was still firm. "But he will. He said he would."

Wendy set two boxes of Cracker Jack on the table. "Mr. Quirk bought me one and I asked for another.

My mother thought that was terrible. But he was glad to give it to me." She finished bleakly, "He'd give me anything, I guess."

Ursula Ma'am turned the Cracker Jack box in her paws. "It's very pretty," she said hesitantly. Then, deciding, "I will put it with the cheerings," she announced brightly. "It will comfort me to look at it."

Otto shook his box. "A rattle thing," he said knowingly. He began to shake the box in rhythm, thumping one paw lightly on the table. *Rattle thump. Rattle thump.*

Wendy couldn't believe what she was hearing. "It's Cracker Jack."

The name meant nothing to the bears.

"You open the box," she explained. "You eat what's inside. Except not the surprise," she added hastily.

Otto got his box open first and emptied the caramel-coated popcorn onto the table. He poked a few pieces into his mouth, looked pleased, and reached for his prize, a small square of folded cardboard. It opened to reveal a set of vividly colored dragons.

"Funny stickers," exclaimed Wendy.

Otto looked puzzled.

She peeled off one of the dragons. "You pull them off and stick them on your books or on your bike or . . ." But Otto didn't have books or a bike!

Otto himself solved the problem. Solemnly he took the sticker and stuck it to one side of his nose. He grinned lopsidedly. "Or on your nose?" he asked.

Wendy giggled.

"Ot-to *dear!*" Ursula Ma'am couldn't help laughing. "I think," she said, "I think it would look better there." She pointed at the valise.

Laughing, Otto stuck the dragons onto the old suit-case.

Like baggage stickers, Wendy thought.

Ursula Maam was turning her surprise in her paws. Wendy bent to look at it. "Why, it's a ring."

A paper ring, it was, with a blue star for a stone. Wendy punched it out of its paper holder and slipped the tabs together to make a circle. "See?"

Ursula Ma'am took it, observing wistfully, "Maybe it's lucky because it's a star. Maybe it means the talk thing will work soon."

But if the ring was lucky, it wasn't noticeably so. The radio didn't work that evening, nor in the days that followed. And Dr. Corrigan didn't call.

Some of Wendy's hardest times were at school.

Kelly and Sara and Wendy had been best friends since preschool. Every minute outside of school they spent together. At night they talked to each other on the phone until someone's mother said, "Don't you see enough of Kelly—or Sara, or Wendy—at school all day?"

Monday morning, during her first free activity,

Wendy settled on the floor in the corner of the class-room Miss Bunchley called the Book Nook. She pulled the "S" volume of the encyclopedia from the shelf and thumbed though it, looking for *static*. Saber . . . Saddle . . . St. Bernard . . .

Like iron to a magnet, Kelly and Sara were drawn to the corner. They plopped down on either side of her.

Kelly spoke thickly around a caramel. "Wow! Look at that!" She poked at the page. "St. Elmo's Fire." She leaned forward, reading. "A flaming phe-no-me-non sometimes seen around ships' masts in stormy weather. Weird!"

"You doing a project on fire, Wendy?" asked Sara, speaking carefully, her lips held stiff to hide her braces.

"Well, not exactly." Wendy felt her ears get hot. She closed the book and yawned elaborately. "Just wanted to know something."

Kelly looked at her searchingly. "Wendy Devlin, you've got a secret. I can always tell. You act super-cool."

Sara's eyes danced. She forgot the braces and they flashed in all their steely brilliance. "You've got to tell. We promised on my great-grandmother's garnet earring we'd always tell each other our secrets."

Wendy pushed at her glasses. It was true they had promised solemnly. But memory of Ursula Ma'am's terrible fear of "humans" was still vivid. She had given her word not to tell. And Ursula Ma'am trusted her.

"I told you when Jason called me Lockjaw and I hid his social studies book under Bunchy's desk," said Sara.

Kelly added her bit. "I told you Mr. Gautier's pants have got knees in them even when he's standing up."

"That's not a secret," protested Wendy.

"You never saw that before," Kelly persisted. "And you laughed."

Sara added to the list. "I told you about my dad's promotion before I was supposed to."

"I told you Todd loves Karen," said Kelly. "And he got mad at me too."

Wendy worried. Somehow this secret was different from others they had shared. So much depended on it. She was caught between two promises. Her pact with Kelly and Sara. And her word given to Ursula Ma'am.

Kelly put on a fiendish look. "We'll follow you, and we'll hound you, and we'll—"

"We'll ask your mother," Sara said quietly.

"No!" The word burst from Wendy. If her mother thought something unusual was happening at the Heywood, she would start worrying, with who knew what consequences.

Kelly preened. "Ha! Gotcha!"

There was no choice. It was better for Kelly and Sara to know than for her mother to find out. "You've got to solemnly promise—"

"We do," they chorused in a hoarse whisper.

"—not to say one single word. You've got to swear not even to talk about it when I'm not with you. You've got—"

"Okay, okay." Kelly sighed impatiently. "We promise."

Wendy looked over her shoulder. Nobody had come into the Book Nook. "There are bears in the apartment over ours," she said softly. "They came Friday morning."

"Bears!" Sara looked scared.

Kelly forgot the caramel she was unpeeling. "You mean Dr. Corrigan's got some cubs up there? But I thought pets weren't allowed in your building."

Wendy shook her head emphatically. "I mean really grown-up bears. Only they're not so big. And they can talk. They came in a taxi, and—"

Kelly fell over on the floor laughing. When she sat up she sketched an imaginary mark on an imaginary blackboard: Score one for Wendy. "You sure had me going!"

Sara looked relieved. "I thought you really meant it, Wendy. Bears!" she scoffed.

Kelly and Sara didn't believe her! How could they not believe her? "But it's true! Their names are—"

"My name is Martha Washington," Kelly announced formally. "My friend here," she nodded at Sara, "is Betsy Ross."

Wendy gave up. *Gladly,* she gave up. Otto and Ursula Ma'am's secret was still safe. And maybe she hadn't really broken her word, since Kelly and Sara didn't believe her.

Miss Bunchley clapped her hands and said it was time for social studies, everybody. Wendy pushed the heavy book onto the encyclopedia shelf and followed the girls back to her seat. Never would she have thought Kelly and Sara wouldn't believe her.

In the days that followed, Wendy looked up more about static, and radios, and transistors. Along the way she learned about vacuum tubes and CB radios and printed circuits—was there anybody anywhere who understood those?—but she didn't find out why there was static on the bears' radio. Or how to fix it.

Things with Kelly and Sara went from stiff, to strained, to absolutely terrible. They had taken to watching her guardedly, exchanging glances when she refused their invitations to go home with them after school as she had always done.

The bell had just rung one afternoon and Wendy was slipping the "R" volume, for rocks, in among her books when Sara saw what she was doing. Her eyes widened. "Wendy! You know we're not allowed to take the encyclopedia out of the room."

"You studying to be a genius or something?" asked Kelly. The words were teasing, but there was an unfriendly undertone to the question.

60

"There's just something I've got to find out. I'll bring it back tomorrow," Wendy said vaguely, arranging her jacket over the books.

"Want to come to my house and listen to Pickle Pete and the Purple Cucumber?" Kelly asked. But she said it coolly, as though she expected Wendy to say no.

"Can't," said Wendy. "I'm—I've got to go to the dentist."

"But you went just last month," protested Sara. "And you didn't have any cavities."

"Maybe you've got some new best friends," Kelly said flatly. "Maybe you just don't want to be best friends with us. Well all right for you, Wendy Devlin."

Sara, looking hurt, turned away. "We just won't bother you anymore."

"But I haven't!" Wendy protested. "You know—" But Kelly and Sara moved away, their heads close.

Wendy's throat felt stiff and it hurt. She swallowed. Never had she felt so lonely.

Waiting for the light to change at Sheridan Road, she eyed the activity around the high-rise under construction on the corner. A steel beam rode up the side of the building, guided from below by hardhats holding ropes.

"—turning the street into a steel-and-concrete canyon."

A conversation was going on next to her.

"Any more of these and the sun'll never get down here to the street," said one of the men.

"Bad for TV reception, too," said the other.

Wendy's attention came into focus. She listened openly.

"Got some interference on Channel Two now," said the first man. "Moved the set three times. The wife says she's tired of changing the furniture around for the TV."

Interference. Was that static? "Uh-uh—"

The men ignored her.

"Mister? What's interference?" She had to speak twice before they heard her.

One of the men looked down. "You say something, sis?"

"What's interference?"

"Ghosts," explained the man. "Snow. The picture flops."

"Does that hurt radios?" That's what she really wanted to know.

The men conferred.

"I don't think so. Don't most of them have built-in antennas?"

"Some do, some don't. You may need a booster. And you might get a little buzz until you find the right spot for it."

Hope bubbled in Wendy. Move the radio! Move it around the apartment!

The men didn't notice her leave. "Yes, but these powerful new radios . . ."

Her eyes dancing, she burst into the apartment. "We've got to move it!"

Otto looked dazed. "What?"

"The radio," said Wendy. "Let's move it around to different rooms. Maybe it'll work better somewhere else."

They tried it in the foyer and there wasn't any difference. Possibly it was better in the bedroom. But it was most certainly better in the living room. And the farther they moved into the room, the less noise came from the radio.

"The windows," exclaimed Wendy. "The closer we get to them, the better it is."

Otto pointed at the cord, extended tautly from the radio to the wall outlet. "Can't get nearer."

"I know how to fix that," Wendy said happily. Minutes later she returned with the extension cord her mother used for ironing. "See? You just plug this into the wall." She did so. "And plug the radio cord into the other end." She did that. "And now we can move it right up to the windows," she finished proudly.

The windows reached from floor to ceiling and the view was free of the new high-rises that were pushing upward to the south along Sheridan Road. Wendy's building was the tallest of the old apartment buildings that sprawled northward. She parted the draperies and the bears nudged the radio close to the windows.

Otto opened the switch, his paw hovering, ready to extinguish the rattling that never came. The panel light glowed. A moment passed, and another. Silent moments. Beautiful, still moments.

"Our talk thing is working," he chortled, adjusting dials.

Ursula Ma'am hurried away and returned with the flute.

Wendy had grown up with music. With her mother's string group. With Sunday concerts at Orchestra Hall. But the music that flowed from Ursula Ma'am's flute was a blending of melodies such as Wendy had never heard.

Do leaves bursting from their budcases in spring toss a song into the air? Do sunsets sing? Wendy heard them. And the swoop and wheel of birds in flight. And the hushed wind rushing through the tops of towering pines.

Otto broke the mood. "What's that?"

Wendy came out of her enchantment. "What?"

Otto's nose twitched.

Only then did she become aware of an acrid odor in the room.

Everything happened at once.

A sound came from the radio. A single, spine-tingling chord that might be from a thousand pipe organs.

A delighted smile curved Ursula Ma'am's lips. *The Others*. She formed the words silently.

A hollow pop came from the wall outlet, a flash of blue-white light. The smell of burning rubber assaulted Wendy's nose. And the music of the Others faded.

Excitedly Otto jiggled the switch.

Nothing happened.

"It's sick again," he moaned. "The talk thing is sick."

"And they were just beginning to tell us—" wailed Ursula Ma'am. She didn't finish saying what the Others had started to tell them.

Chapter 7

As the days passed, with the radio stubbornly mute and with no call from Dr. Corrigan, the bears began to show the strain of living with trouble.

Otto prowled restlessly through the apartment, humming softly, a brave sound. He seemed to be telling himself if he acted cheerful everything would be all right.

From the living room, shielded by the draperies, he looked down on the roof gardens, on shrubs and trees in tubs. One of the gardens even had vegetables, lettuce and tomatoes and corn planted in cartons and cans and containers of every description.

"Strange," Otto rumbled absently. Then, "Poor humans." A sigh. "A mountain's a sight better."

Aimlessly, wandering to the den, murmuring, "I feel so locked up," he would look off to the east at the park. Fall was in full, sweet richness now, the trees a necklace of flaming color edging the blue curve of the lagoon. He admired the trees. But it was the grass that interested him most.

"Good, soft prickly grass," he observed one day. He

66

rubbed the flat of one foot against the fur of the other ankle. "Feet do like the tickle of it. Don't know how humans stand such hard stuff on the feet."

Wendy looked down at her own bare feet. She didn't much know either. She liked to go barefoot, and grass was much, much nicer than sidewalks. Humans were, if not strange, at least less given to pure comfort than bears. Maybe bears knew something humans didn't. . . .

On tiptoe, craning his neck for the best view, Otto stared down at the lagoon. "Got to be fish in that pond. Not the shimmery kind. They like fast water. But good, white fish." He licked his lips. "The human kind"—he meant the canned fish in Dr. Corrigan's cupboard— "are good. But you can't beat a fish you just picked up in the water."

He wore a look of such dreamy contentment at the memory that Wendy had to believe you couldn't.

The uncertainty of the future told on Ursula Ma'am too. She roamed the apartment, picking up things and setting them down, always in a different spot. A squat stone eskimo was picked up from an end table, warmed between her paws, studied, and placed on one of the lower bookshelves. A gilded and lacquered Russian box was opened, examined, and moved from bookshelf to windowsill. A piece of scrimshaw was stroked, turned, and came to rest finally on the coffee table.

"It's so the same here. All the time," mused Ursula Ma'am, "so forever the same."

Its lack of sameness in recent days had troubled Wendy. Hans or Felix could come in. They might notice things out of place and know for sure someone was here. And yet she hadn't spoken. The bears didn't need something else to worry them.

Still, the danger was real, and this seemed a good opening.

"Things don't move around inside apartments," she pointed out. "If they do, you know somebody has moved them."

Ursula Ma'am didn't respond to the logic of that. She spun the globe on its walnut stand and watched it move. "On the mountain, things are never the same." Spin. "Leaves fall and skip away in the wind. Waterfalls run full after a rain and only trickle after all the water has gone down the mountain. All day the shadows move around behind the trees, hiding from the sun." Spin. "The mountain, it's always changing."

Wendy had been listening closely, thinking. "But some things don't change," she protested. "They really don't. Rock doesn't. And aren't mountains made of rock?"

Ursula Ma'am looked at her directly. "It changes. Rain and snow wear it away. And the great cold reaches deep into it and cracks it open. When you wake up winters in the deep cold, and your ear is near the ground, you hear it, the cracks and snaps of the mountain changing." She set the globe spinning, then stopped it abruptly with her paw. "In the first warmth, seeds put their roots down into the cracks and the rock opens still more.

"The mountain changes." Her eyes met Wendy's. "And that's what makes it beautiful."

Wendy didn't try to explain further about not moving things around in the apartment. Some uncertainties you just had to live with.

There were other talks that week too. Mostly about humans.

"Who are they?" Otto asked, staring down at Sheridan Road from the window in the den.

Wendy leaned on the sill, looking at the people hurrying at the crosswalks. "Don't know," she said idly.

"Don't know!" Otto was shocked.

"There are too many people in the city to know them all," Wendy added.

"We knew all the bears on the mountain." Otto made of it a highly desirable thing, to know all bears. "They were our friends. We were theirs."

But you couldn't possibly know everybody in a city!

"Cities aren't so nice for humans," concluded Ursula Ma'am. "Poor humans."

Wendy wasn't sure she liked being felt sorry for.

Another time, "Where are they all going?" asked Ursula Ma'am. "All the humans down there. They walk so fast."

"It's the rush hour," said Wendy.

Ursula Ma'am was stunned. "Humans have a time to rush!"

"No. No. It's called that because everyone's coming or going at the same time. They're mostly going home."

"To cooped-up places like this?" Again the note of sympathy.

"Mostly," Wendy admitted. "There are lots of apartments in this neighborhood. And some of those people are maybe going to the supermarket for food."

"We just picked it up, our food, on the mountain," said Otto. "Fish. Berries."

Ursula Ma'am wouldn't let it go. "Where else do they go?"

"Well . . ." Wendy had to think. "Kids go to school in the morning."

The bears exchanged a look. "That's where they learn to act like humans," Otto said knowingly. Then, to Wendy, "Our young just follow their dam and they learn about food and snow and rain."

Wendy did her best. "Human children need to know lots more than that."

The bears waited.

"We learn to write," she said. "And spell. And read."

Reading. That had its effect, for the bears had discovered Dr. Corrigan's books. They pored over the pictures and sometimes asked Wendy to explain them.

"That is a good human thing," Ursula Ma'am conceded.

"If we stayed a long time here, we could go to school and learn to read," Otto agreed.

For the most part, the bears rated human customs as bad, sad, or good. Big cities and fences were bad. Humans living all "cooped up" and not knowing each other was sad. A few things were good. Reading was one of those. So were fire trucks and fire fighters.

The sirens and ominous roar of the powerful engines had at first frightened the bears. But when Wendy told them what fire fighters did, they looked thoughtful.

"Saw a fire on the mountain once." Otto's voice roughened. "A terrible thing."

"The humans who put out fires are a good thing," declared Ursula Ma'am.

Wendy was pleased that a few things human met with their approval.

Wendy was becoming well-acquainted with the contents of the valise. Each day yielded some fresh wonder.

There was a pawful of pine needles, and she knew without asking that more were stowed away in the valise. She sifted them through her fingers. "Like under the Christmas tree!" she exclaimed delightedly. Then, a frown creased her forehead. "But they'll spoil."

Ursula Ma'am, her head to one side, looked at her quizzically. "Spoil? Why 'spoil,' child?"

"Well, I mean" —and even as she spoke Wendy suspected she was saying something that would mean nothing to bears— "they'll get brown and dry and what'll you do then?"

The answer was simple. "Keep them." But trying to explain the answer wasn't simple. Ursula Ma'am held her cupped paws to receive the pine needles. She stared into them, "reading" her answer. "All things change. Sometimes the changing makes you happy and sometimes it makes you sad." She held the pine needles to her nose and breathed deeply of their fragrance. "But it's meant to be. I loved them in the beginning. I will go on loving them."

It was a long speech for Ursula Ma'am. She poured the pine needles back into the valise and withdrew a collection of bark for Wendy's inspection.

Here were the brown, mottled bark of the ponderosa pine, the orange brown of yellow pine, the reddish brown, sweetly scented bark of the juniper cedar, the white bark of the young aspen. Shaggy, spongy, hard and ridged, smooth—all kinds of bark from trees on the mountain. Each piece was tagged, the name printed in the familiar bold hand.

Wonderingly, Wendy fingered them. So! Bark was not just any old kind of rough covering on a tree. Each tree had its own "fingerprint." It was an idea that took getting used to.

The valise also contained a book, bulky, sturdy, firmly strapped. Each page held an artfully arranged dried flower, neatly taped into place, and a lumpy seed-filled envelope.

"Our gift to the Others," explained Ursula Ma'am. She smiled. "If there's nothing on that Brūn, there will be. And then the Others will know how dear our mountain was."

Otto touched the lettering on a page. "Dr. Corrigan, he helped us. Somebody there on that Brūn will know what the marks mean."

Dr. Corrigan. Where was he? Three days passed, and a fourth. The bears had to report that the phone never rang.

And the "sick" radio sat in the living room, the cord coiled beside it, concealed by the draperies. From time to time Otto plugged it into the wall outlet. But the effort was useless. It didn't work.

Before long, the bears showed symptoms Wendy recognized. She remembered the first time she stayed at Grandpa's without her mother. As daylight faded and shadows reached across the pasture toward the house, a fear and an end-of-the-world feeling had overcome her.

Ursula Ma'am put it rightly one afternoon as the lowering sun washed the sides of buildings with gold. "I've got such an all-gone feeling," she murmured.

She didn't even notice the cheerings. And they were spread out on the coffee table right in front of her.

Chapter 8

That night Wendy stared unseeing at her math book. What would make Otto and Ursula Ma'am feel nicer? She doodled a funny face into a figure 8, added ears and a tail, and the 8 turned into a sitting cat. Impatiently scratching it out, she tried to imagine the mountain. What was there? Rain. And air. And trees. And food—fish and berries, for sure.

She remembered the time she had had the measles and spent a whole week indoors and how good the air smelled the first time she went outside. She recalled playing under the fountain spray at the pool. The memories led to an idea. She emptied out her bank and counted her savings.

After school the next day she stopped at the Shop and Save. Adding as she went, she bought apples and pears. They would taste good. She picked out a pumpkin, just for fun. Maybe she would carve a face in it. She ignored the vegetables. No vegetables tasted good.

She bought peanut butter, because Otto and Ursula Ma'am had taken such a liking to it. She paused in front of the honey—bears liked honey. Or—did they?

Otto and Ursula Ma'am weren't like any bears she had ever read about. Still . . . she added the honey to her shopping cart.

Recalling Otto's talk about the fish in the "pond," she stopped at the Cape Cod counter, where fish swam around in a tank and you picked out the one you wanted. She chose the smallest and waited to see what it would cost.

It was somehow awesome, to see the fish alive and swimming around one minute, and to have it—wrapped up in a package with a price written on it in heavy black pencil—handed across the counter a few minutes later.

She added things up and counted her money. There wasn't enough. She leaned over the cart. The pumpkin was fun, but it wasn't something bears usually had to have. She sighed and returned it to the produce section.

At the checkout counter she found her addition had been wrong, but in her favor. She got fifty-seven cents back in change.

"I sure can't do this very much," she thought as she trudged home, pulling her mother's shopping cart.

Joe opened the street door for her and held it while she maneuvered the cart into the lobby. "Well now, if you just aren't getting to be a real nice help to your mama!"

It was the kind of talk Wendy detested, as though someone were patting her on the head. And besides, she wanted nothing so much as to be invisible when she did something for Otto and Ursula Ma'am. She replied with an unfriendly grunt.

Joe, a nice man who had known her since she rode a tricycle, looked surprised and hurt. Wendy felt guilty. She really did like Joe. "Sorry I was grumpy, Joe. I guess I've caught the awkward age."

Joe laughed and held the inner lobby door for her.

Upstairs, the bears' spirits were buoyed by the food. They bit into the apples and admired the pears. Their eyes sparkled when they saw the fish.

"You caught it down in that pond," Otto said excitedly.

"Uh-uh." Wendy tried to explain about the fish tank at the Shop and Save.

Bleakness sounded in Ursula Ma'am's voice. "All cooped up. Not free. Poor things."

Hurriedly Wendy changed the subject.

"Come on. We're going to open a window in every room, just a little bit. The fresh air will make you feel good."

They trailed after her with excited little skips. Something was happening at last. Something different was breaking up the sameness.

Crisp autumn air flowed through the apartment. Otto grinned. "Nice, nice, nice." Like a gourmet sniffing seasoning in the soup, he sampled it more carefully. "Not as good as mountain air. Seem to be little things floating in it." Then, remembering his manners—Wendy was after all one of the humans who sheltered him and this was her air—he added lamely, "Well, of course, it *is* passable. Lacks sparkle, you might say, but passable. . . ."

Wendy wasn't fooled. She wondered what made mountain air different. But she would have to think about that later, because she had another surprise for Otto and Ursula Ma'am.

Pausing at the linen closet to gather towels, which were the nice, extra big kind, just right for someone as tall as Dr. Corrigan, she led the way to the bathroom.

Otto and Ursula Ma'am poked their noses over her shoulders, watching curiously as she marked the cold water tap in the shower stall with a dab of her mother's red nail polish. She blew on it to dry it.

"There." She stepped back, bumping into Ursula Ma'am, who bumped into Otto as they danced out of her way. She closed the shower door most of the way, reached in cautiously, and turned on the water.

A smile of purest pleasure spread over Otto's face. "A waterfall!"

Paws clasped, Ursula Ma'am surveyed this human wonder. "It sounds so homey!" She brushed past Wendy and stepped under the water, face turned up to it, eyes closed. She wore a look of pure bliss.

Otto hopped up and down. "Me next. Me next."

Ursula Ma'am moved back so he could get under the spray.

Hands on her hips, Wendy grinned at their delight. "Only use the handle I marked," she warned. "And be sure to turn it off when you finish."

Playing and splashing, the bears were having so much fun Wendy almost wished she were a bear! Their laughter was the happiest sound she had heard in days.

They didn't even notice when she left.

Over meat loaf and carrots that evening, her mother announced she was going out. "I'll ask Mrs. Tulippe to look in on you," she added.

"Aw, Mom," Wendy moaned. "I don't need to be put to bed. I'm not an infant."

"Well." Her mother considered. "I suppose you are old enough to be alone for an evening. If you promise not to open the door, we'll try it this time."

"You're going out with that Mr. Quirk," Wendy said accusingly.

"Only to a concert, darling." Her mother set aside the dinner plates and took pineapple divinity from the refrigerator. "It's nothing to get upset about."

"Who's upset!" Wendy yelled.

Her mother chose to overlook her bad temper. "I'll be home early."

Wendy ignored the pineapple divinity, her most favorite dessert. "I'll bet Mr. Quirk doesn't know a—

a—French horn from a flute. I'll bet he doesn't even like music."

"Now you just don't know that," her mother suggested reasonably.

Wendy insisted. "He's only pretending to like it because you do."

A note of weariness crept into her mother's voice. "As a matter of fact, he is a fine violinist. Really, dear, your dislike of poor Peter is quite unreasoning. You don't dislike Chad or Felicia or Rob"—they were the members of her string group—"and Peter does try to be so nice to you."

Wendy didn't answer. She dug into the pineapple divinity. Something had to make her feel nicer. Maybe pineapple divinity would do it.

She was curled up on the sofa watching TV when Mr. Quirk arrived. She peeked. He was wearing blue tonight. A blue tie. And go-along socks, of course.

She peeked again and was relieved not to see an eyeball tie tack staring at her from his tie.

"Well, hello, chum. And how's school?" he asked heartily.

The question was so predictable it didn't deserve much of an answer. "Okay."

"Lookee." He reached into an inner pocket. "I brought you something." He dropped a tangle of connected metal rings on the coffee table. "A puzzle from the mysterious East."

Wendy picked it up, but her eyes weren't on the puzzle. They were riveted to his hand. Mr. Quirk was wearing a pinky ring. And the stone in it was a blue eyeball!

"Wendy?" her mother prodded. "What do you say?"

"Thanks," mumbled Wendy. She stared pointedly at her mother and back at Mr. Quirk's hand. But her mother wasn't tuned in to signals tonight. As a matter of fact, she looked disapproving. Wendy gave up and tried to work up a little polite enthusiasm. "It's pretty neat."

Mr. Quirk looked pleased with himself. "Bet you a Coke you can't get it apart before I see you again."

Wendy didn't answer. She just tossed the puzzle from hand to hand, hoping fervently there wouldn't be a next time.

Her mother kissed her, and Wendy let them out, locking the door after them.

Absentmindedly, watching the end of "Harbor Patrol," she took apart the puzzle and dropped the rings on the coffee table. Nothing to it. Mr. Quirk's puzzle was practically an insult to anybody with even half a head.

She turned off the TV and went to her room. Undoing the heavy gold of her braid, she stood brushing her hair, studying a picture on the chest of drawers. Her father was laughing and pushing her on a swing. She remembered that day. Her mother had taken the picture. Afterward the three of them had fed peanuts to the squirrels.

She leaned close to the picture, examining the blurred face of the child. She had been really little, then. And she had had pigtails instead of her queue. Thoughtfully, her eyes still on the picture, she parted her hair and began to braid it into pigtails. She had to dig around in her top drawer to find a rubber band to fasten the second one. Snapping the elastic into place, she compared the face in the mirror with the one in the photograph. After a moment she rummaged through another drawer and withdrew a blue granny gown that had once been her favorite. She slid it over her head.

Startled, she looked down at herself.

The gown ended three inches above her ankles. Her wrists stuck too far out of the sleeves. And the gown pulled across her shoulders. She shrugged, as though that could make it looser.

She carried the picture to her bedside table and set it next to a green plaster frog she had made. She stared at the faces for another long moment before slipping between the sheets and turning off the light. Daddy . . .

Yawning, she started to take off her glasses, then thought better of it. Not for a while. The lights were blurry without her glasses.

Looking out at the night city, she thought about her father and felt warm and cozy. Somehow Mr. Quirk

got into her thoughts, and then she felt sour and unhappy. She pushed him out of her mind and thought
about her father some more.

A plane on its landing path to O'Hare cut across
the sky.

Wendy's eyes opened, closed. The lights brightened,
dimmed.

She bunched up the pillow under her cheek, turning
her glasses askew. She had forgotten about the glasses.

A wispy fog drifted into the city, veiling the lights.

Wendy slept.

She was awakened by a tapping at her window.

Tap . . . tap . . . tap . . . tap . . .

Chapter 9

Uncertain of what had awakened her, Wendy lay on her side, a rigid, huddled lump under the blue-flowered comforter. Something wasn't right.

Unmoving, she let her eyes sweep the room. Nothing had changed since last night, except that darkness had given way to light. The far wall was burnished by the sun.

Tap . . . tap-tap-tap . . .

The sound came from behind her. On the twenty-fourth floor of her apartment building, something, someone, was knocking at her window!

A chill fingered its way up her spine, tightening her scalp. Whatever was there, good or bad, she must look.

Cautiously, still huddled with her back to the window, she reached for her glasses on the bedside table. They weren't there. She remembered then, and searched between the sheets. She had to bend them to make them fit when she found them. Clutching her comforter, only her eyes showing above it—as though that could protect her—she rolled over.

Outside the window, teased by a gentle wind, a pine-cone hung suspended by a length of tousled rope. *Tap-tap*. It brushed the glass.

She let out her breath and relaxed her grip on the comforter. How dumb to have been so scared! Of course nobody could knock on her window way up here. It was only—Otto? Ursula Ma'am?

She shot upright.

Something was wrong. Otto and Ursula Ma'am wouldn't risk attracting attention if something important wasn't happening.

On silent toes she darted to her door and eased it shut. She had trouble with the window, which always stuck, but finally managed a space wide enough to get her head through. Twisting awkwardly, she looked upward.

Nothing was there except the roof lights, pale globes against the blue cup of the sky. The bears weren't looking down from the window above.

She gave the rope a hearty jerk and was rewarded immediately by an answering tug. Then the rope snaked slowly upward and disappeared.

"Hey, Otto?" Softly. No answer. Louder. "Ursula Ma'am?"

Still there was no reply.

After an uncertain moment, she wriggled back inside and closed the window.

The clock said 6:30. Any time now her mother's

radio would go on. There was no way she could escape before breakfast.

Nor did she.

She had to sit through the whole, long, everlasting meal before she could ask to be excused. What's more, it was one of her mother's firm mornings. Wendy was sent firmly to her room to make her bed before she left for school. She was sent, firmly once more, back to her room to change out of the tennis shoes she liked best into new ones that hardly had a mark on them. Then her mother, firmly, insisted on looking over the math problems Wendy had done before dinner last night. And when she thought she had just about made it to freedom, her math book under her arm, her hand on the doorknob, her mother's voice stopped her.

"Wendy? You're going out the *kitchen* door?"

Wendy froze.

Nobody ever used the back entrance. The service elevator was reserved for deliveries, and there was no way to the ground floor except down twenty-four flights of stairs. Her mind did flip-flops. "I'm doing a . . . a project." True. She was. With the bears. "Uh, on transportation." A little less than true. "I'm counting the steps." And she would too. All the way upstairs.

Her mother returned to her coffee. "I'll have to unearth your old abacus."

Wendy ran back and kissed her, to make up for the

fibs. Then she let herself out into the hall.

The kitchen door upstairs opened even before she finished knocking. Ursula Ma'am faced her, eyes deeply blue and troubled, paws pressed to her breast. "It's Otto." The soft voice quivered. "He went out there." She gestured vaguely toward the outdoors beyond the window.

Wendy felt the way she had once when a softball hit her in the stomach and she couldn't catch her breath.

"Right before sunup." Ursula Ma'am held her paws to her lips, unable to continue. Then, "Said he was going to that pond to get some fish before the humans got there. Only the sun is up, and now it's full light." The next words were a soft wail. "And he didn't come back!"

Images raced through Wendy's mind. Of Otto being chased by unfriendly humans. Of Otto hiding somewhere, unable to find his way back to the Heywood.

Ursula Ma'am straightened, pursed her lips, let out her breath in a little puff of air, and turned to the red plaid coat draped over a chair. "I'm going to find him."

"Oh, but wait! You can't," Wendy begged. It was bad enough to have Otto in danger. The thought of Ursula Ma'am wandering around in the park was just too much.

Ursula Ma'am was buttoning herself into the coat. "I looked down there. I saw a path. I'll just follow that

86

path to the pond, and—"

"Wait. I know all about the park," Wendy pleaded. "More than you do. I'll find him."

Ursula Ma'am's resolve wavered.

"How was he dressed?" Wendy corrected herself. "I mean, *was* he dressed?"

Ursula Ma'am nodded vigorously. "Human clothes, like when we came." The thought cheered her. "He looks real human, dressed like that. Maybe the humans won't notice him."

The jangle of the wall phone shattered the hush of the kitchen. Unnaturally loud in the uncurtained, uncarpeted room, the sound bounced off walls, stove, refrigerator.

Their startled eyes on the telephone, neither Wendy nor Ursula Ma'am moved. Then hope flowed between them like sunbeams cutting through clouds. Dr. Corrigan!

Ursula Ma'am pointed at the noisy thing. "You . . . I never—I never . . . You talk into it."

Wendy grabbed the phone. "Hello? Is that you, Dr. Corrigan?"

There was silence. Then, "Who is this?" The kind, gravelly voice, usually so authoritative, registered confusion. "Ursula Ma'am? No. Um. Who is this?"

"I knew it would be you," crowed Wendy. "It's me, Dr. Corrigan. Wendy."

"Wendy! What are you doing there?"

Wendy didn't answer. "Wait. Here's Ursula Ma'am."

With trembling paws Ursula Ma'am took the phone. "Dr. Corrigan—" She was speaking into the wrong end of it. Wendy righted it and put it back in her paws. "Like that," she whispered.

"Oh, Dr. Corrigan." The words tumbled out. "The talk thing doesn't work. It all stopped. And Otto's gone. And I don't know what to do."

She listened, speaking around pauses. "Yes. Yes. It's there. I'll get it. She's here." Mutely she offered the phone to Wendy and hurried out of the kitchen.

"Hello?"

"Wendy, tell me from the beginning. What's going on there?"

Wendy did. Everything right up to Otto and this morning. "I'm scared," she finished softly, looking over her shoulder to be sure Ursula Ma'am hadn't come back into the kitchen.

"All right now." The gruff voice was reassuring. "You can be scared, but don't let Ursula Ma'am know that. We'll fix things as best we can."

Wendy listened.

"Otto's got to be found and brought back, of course. That's going to be up to you. But before you go out, do a couple of things.

"You said the radio worked well enough in the living room?"

"Uh-huh." Remembering, Wendy's nose wrinkled.

"There was this funny smell, like stewing rubber."

"Go and disconnect the radio from the wall socket." How wonderful to have somebody telling her what to do! "And on your way, try the kitchen light."

She left the phone swinging on its cord, thumping against the wall. She nearly collided at the door with Ursula Ma'am, carrying the green ring binder.

As she expected, the radio cord was coiled behind the draperies, unplugged. Otto was careful about that, in case "those humans" came back into the apartment.

On her way back into the kitchen she flipped the light switch. Nothing happened. In passing, she opened and shut the refrigerator. The interior was unexpectedly dark.

Ursula Ma'am was talking to Dr. Corrigan. "On the page after the talk thing page?" She was quiet briefly, listening, then handed the phone to Wendy.

"The radio's not plugged in," Wendy reported. "And the kitchen light doesn't work. Neither does the one in the fridge."

"That explains things, I think." The words were measured, unhurried. Wendy began to catch the calmness. "Wendy, do you know what a circuit breaker is?"

"Uh-uh."

"There's a little door in the wall next to the refrigerator. Open it. See if one of the switches in there is out of line with the rest in any one row. If it is, push it into line. Then try the light."

Wendy found the box. Was there one like it downstairs? Funny. She had never noticed.

Sure enough, one of the switches was out of place. She snapped it into alignment. The kitchen light went on and the refrigerator set up a reassuring hum.

She ran back to the phone. "It worked. The light's on." Holding the phone at arm's length, she reached across the room and opened the refrigerator. "The light's on in the fridge now too."

"I thought so. You overloaded a circuit," Dr. Corrigan explained. "Now, one more item before you leave. Ursula Ma'am has the book open to the page where I showed them how to assemble an antenna."

Ursula Ma'am, next to her, was patiently holding the book open to a drawing of a spidery angled thing.

The deliberate voice continued. "The parts for it are in the side pocket of one of the suitcases. See if you can find them."

Again the phone was left dangling. Wendy returned in a moment, clutching a handful of metal strips. "Got 'em."

"Good girl. Now you lay those out on the floor next to the radio just the way they're shown in the drawing. Ursula Ma'am can start screwing the pieces together."

Wendy returned to the living room with an anxious Ursula Ma'am trotting behind her, still carrying the book. "Tell me what to do, child."

90

"Hold it, like this." Wendy tilted the pages. "So I can see."

She crawled around between the coffee table and the chairs, laying out the metal pieces, looking up from time to time at the drawing. There seemed to be a screw and nut for each joint. She put them beside the holes.

Ursula Ma'am was alert. "I see," she murmured. "I see!" She propped the book against a chair. "I remember." She screwed two of the strips together. Brightening, she said quietly, "I can do this."

Wendy watched for a moment. Yes, Ursula Ma'am did seem to have the hang of it. She got up. "I'm going for Otto now."

Ursula Ma'am paused in her work. "I will put this together. And when you come, and Otto"—she seemed to stroke his name as she said it—"it will be all finished."

"I'll try to be quick," Wendy assured her, heading for the kitchen.

"Child?"

Wendy turned.

Fear still haunted Ursula Ma'am's eyes. But she said, with quiet dignity, "May the one among the Others we most honor, the Great Ursus, protect you."

As she had that first morning so long ago, Wendy wanted to curtsey. But she didn't. "Thank you, love," was all she said, and, "I'll find him. Don't worry. I'll bring him back."

At the phone, she told Dr. Corrigan what was happening.

"Fine. That'll keep her occupied while you're gone." Concern entered his voice. "Wendy?"

"Yes."

"I'll call every hour on the hour until you're back there with Otto. Now, on your way. Good luck."

Wendy replaced the phone in its cradle.

Never had she felt so absolutely, desperately alone. The future of Ursula Ma'am and Otto and those other bears speeding through space toward the earth rested on her shoulders.

She stood tall. "I'll find Otto," she thought. "I will."

It was a promise to herself.

Chapter 10

The jogging path was cindery and it crunched under the wheels of her five-speed bike, but it was free of ruts and Wendy skimmed along, the wind cool on her hot cheeks. The morning gave promise of a golden autumn day.

Even though it was a weekday, a few joggers were out, pounding along the path. So were the dogs. Some walked sedately on leads. Others bounded free, trailing their leashes while their owners strolled, watching.

Her eyes swept the open green beyond the pedestrian path. Nowhere was there a sign of Otto.

Dear old Otto! Where was he in this immense park? Had someone seen him and called a policeman? She shuddered at the thought of the sweet-natured bear trying to explain to some startled human about the mountain, about himself and Ursula Ma'am, and the Others.

The path stretched before her, an ebony ribbon threading through the green of the grass. Trees arched overhead, their leaves a canopy of crimson and orange and yellow. The path was color-splashed with leaves.

Her eyes lifted. Nobody up there. These weren't good climbing trees. The trunks were either too skinny, or too fat, with even the lowest branches high above the ground.

Off to the left was a clump of bushes. A great place to hide!

Standing on the pedals, she left the path and rolled bumpily over the grass, circling the bushes, calling.

"Otto?" Her eyes probed the greenery. "You in there, Otto?"

She could see he wasn't though. There were just lots of peanut shells and weather-stained candy wrappings.

Back on the path, she passed the driving range. Nothing. And the concession stand. No Otto.

She rode in a wide curve around the park department storeroom. Two small children were swinging in the play lot nearby. They slowed to a stop, their feet dangling, as they watched her search bushes and look up into trees.

"Otto?" she called softly. "Where are you, anyway?"

"Love," somebody called from nearby. It wasn't Otto. The voice came from the tennis courts and it was followed by the ringing plop of lobbed tennis balls.

The lagoon, fed from the lake by a narrow canal under the Outer Drive, reached a long bent arm into the park. It was divided neatly in half by a bridge over which traffic flowed from the Drive, through the park, to the zoo, and beyond to surrounding apartment buildings. Pleasure boats were moored in the north lagoon. The south end was taken over by canoeists and kayakers and fishermen.

Wendy kept to the jogging trail. Around the curve of the lagoon. Past deserted parking lots. Looking. Calling softly.

"Otto. Oh, Otto."

No reply. Nothing.

Ahead, the path crossed a public access road leading down to the boat ramp. She let one foot drop to the path and waited, fingering her queue, while a station wagon towing a cabin cruiser on a trailer inched up the incline and turned onto Cannon Drive.

Ahead, on the other side of the road, a black-and-tan dog romped under the clumped trees that edged the path. Its owner was nowhere in sight.

She stood, pushing at her glasses, biting her lip. Darn! The dog was a really big one. And the way it was bounding around . . . well, it could just as easily come bounding after her.

Maybe if she went down to the boat slips and checked out the boats first, the dog would be gone when she got back. . . .

A squirrel cut directly in front of her, moving in graceful springing leaps, heading toward the row of trees. It sighted the dog. Without altering its pace, it swerved and ran smoothly up a nearby oak.

The dog!

Her attention zeroed in on the dog. Was it just playing, as she had supposed? Alert now, she watched.

The animal's movements all centered around the biggest willow, one that branched out in a cluster from its base. While she watched, the dog stood up, its forepaws on the trunk, barking, showing its teeth.

With growing certainty, Wendy rode toward the tree and looked up.

Overhead, almost concealed by the foliage, his striped coat and white cowboy hat tinted amber by the warm light filtering through the leaves, was Otto. He pushed back his hat and grinned crookedly. "Hello, child. I thought you would never-r-r get her-r-re." His *r*'s were rough, although the words were calm enough.

"Otto!" Wendy's voice trembled with relief. "Ursula Ma'am was so scared. Why'd you go and do such a noodle-y thing?"

He rubbed his nose with the back of a paw. "Seemed like a good enough idea at the time," he said without excitement. "Would have got back without any tr-r-rouble, except for-r-r that one." He pointed at the dog. A wry note entered his voice. "He can't be r-r-r-easoned with, that one."

The puzzled dog dropped to all four feet and backed

away, baring its teeth at Wendy. Low sounds came from deep in its throat.

Not a friendly type of dog at all! Wendy shuddered. But there was only one thing to do. She kept her voice low, talking to Otto. "I'll get him to follow me. When he does, you head for home. Try to look natural. I mean, act like everyone else. I'll catch up with you back near the driving range—that place with the fence around it."

Riding slowly, she circled the tree, whistling, wheedling. "Here, boy. Come with Wendy."

The dog took an uncertain step.

"Thata boy."

Another step.

"Good dog. Come on, boy."

The dog made up its mind. It turned back to the tree, barking hoarsely.

Otto weighed the situation. "It's hungr-r-ry, I guess. It wants a little bite of something to eat—me!" He chuckled nervously.

But that was it: Food!

"Wait," Wendy called. "I'm going home. Be ready to run when I come back. I won't be long."

Nor was she. Fifteen minutes later she was spinning back along the path. In her bike basket, loosely wrapped in paper toweling, lay a pound of sirloin steak. Around it was fastened a sturdy length of twine.

Her mother was going to go into shock about to-night's missing dinner. Wendy shook the thought from her mind. There were more important things to worry about at the moment.

The dog lay in the dappled shade under the tree, its nose on its paws, its eyes wary.

"Here I come," she called. "Ready?"

"R-r-ready," came the rumbling reply.

The dog rose to its feet, its nose twitching.

Wendy rode slowly, circling the tree. She swung the meat in a gentle arc. The delicious scent drifted downwind.

With a yelp of delight, the dog leaped.

But Wendy was ahead of it, racing toward the bike underpass at Fullerton Avenue. Beyond it, she had only to cut kitty-corner to the zoo approach and the gate.

She pedaled furiously, not looking back.

She could hear the dog behind her, breathing heavily, wanting the meat that dangled so temptingly near. The hair on Wendy's neck rose. It was not pleas-ant to feel like the fox in a hunt.

She bent into the wind for more speed.

Get there.

Get to the zoo.

That's all she had to do.

The dog's breathing was louder. She risked a quick

glance over her shoulder. He was gaining on her! He could run faster than she could ride.

She wasn't going to make it to the underpass . . . couldn't . . . couldn't . . .

What was she going to *do?*

Cut across Fullerton Avenue? The morning rush hour was at its peak. Moving cars formed a solid wall between her and the zoo.

But she had to get to the zoo. Had to!

And then, astonishingly, she could.

The cars slowed and stopped for the light at the corner.

Quick. Off the path. Head for the street.

Hurry. Get between those cars before they started moving again. She darted among them.

She had forgotten about cars in the oncoming lane. Tires squealed. Horns blared.

Not breathing, she bounced up and over the curb and cut across the grass, heading toward the zoo approach.

There! She started breathing.

She might have made it all the way to the gate too. Except that ahead of her a police car pulled to the curb, blocking her way.

She slowed.

Instantly the dog was beside her, leaping.

As a cowboy might toss a lariat, she swung the meat

in a circle overhead and let go. It sailed away and was caught fast by the drooping branches of a slender tree.

The police officer was built like a block of granite. His face was expressionless. He stood directly in front of Wendy, his hands on his hips, looking from her to the dog. "Well now, sis, you almost got turned into one flat little girl just now in all that traffic. And your dog with you. Not to speak of almost piling up a couple of cars. Suppose you just tell me how you figure you can go around breaking laws like that."

Chapter 11

"Car twelve . . . *crackle* . . . six . . . *rattle* . . . teen West . . . *crackle* . . . Avenue." A bored voice droned from the raspy radio in the patrol car. From the intersection tires swished, horns beeped. The black-and-tan dog panted heavily under the meat-hung bush. Wendy stood amid the sounds, pushing at a stone in the grass with the toe of a red tennis shoe. She had wanted help. But she had not thought about breaking laws. She had never broken a law before. She didn't know what to say.

The police officer lifted his cap and rubbed at his very shiny bald head. "Let's start with an easy one. Why isn't your dog on a leash?"

"But that's not my dog!" The words burst from Wendy.

"He had Otto up a tree." Mention of his name brought Otto's good-natured face into her mind. Would the officer sense anything strange about an "Otto"? She darted a scared look upward.

The man showed nothing more than sober interest.

She swallowed. "So I went and got the meat and led the dog here so Otto could go the other way."

"Not your dog, huh? Let's have a look at his registration." He started across the grass to inspect the animal's collar. It turned, displaying an impressive mouthful of teeth.

The policeman changed his mind. "Hey, Herb," he called to his partner in the car. "Tell Animal Welfare to get on over here before this sweet-tempered beast starts on somebody's leg."

He came back to Wendy. "Ever hear of traffic laws? They're for kids as well as cars. Tell me how you cross a street."

"Look both ways," mumbled Wendy.

"And? Where do you cross?"

"At the corner."

"When?"

Wendy squirmed. "When the light turns green."

The next question was a jolting one. "Aren't you supposed to be in school?"

She bit her lip. "I'm going. As soon as Otto and I get back home"—actually, she hadn't even thought of school—"to pick up my math book."

The police officer rubbed his chin, studying her. "If I let you go, you'll be careful about your bike in traffic?"

"Yes, sir." It was a whisper.

"And you'll get organized and get yourself and Otto to school?"

She was simply going to die if he didn't stop talking. She looked up beseechingly.

He made up his mind and pulled a pad and pencil from his shirt pocket. "Now you tell me your name and address and where you go to school and then we'll send you on your way."

She was just finishing when the Animal Welfare truck pulled up behind the patrol car. Not waiting to see what they did with the black-and-tan dog, feeling as though Plymouth Rock had been lifted from her shoulders, she sped away. She was careful to cross at the intersection. With the green light. After looking in both directions.

All she had to do now was find Otto, wherever he had taken himself, and hope he wasn't in more trouble.

She needn't have worried.

Look natural, she had cautioned. *Try to act like everyone else.*

And that's precisely what Otto was doing.

She passed the boat ramp, the boarded-up concession stand, the deserted driving range. Otto came into view on the path ahead. Elbows pumping, knees lifted high in the best style, he was jogging!

A runner passed him, then slowed, looking over his shoulder in openmouthed amazement at the undersized figure in the fuzzy, striped blanket coat and white cowboy hat.

Laughter bubbled in Wendy. Otto knew how to take care of himself. He was trying to blend into the surroundings. And he might have. If it weren't for that coat and hat.

She slid to a stop on the path beside him. "Wanna drag?" she asked out of the corner of her mouth the way the boys at school did.

Head tilted, Otto peered out at her from under the broad brim of the hat. Then, alert, he looked around behind her, searching for the dog.

"He's gone," Wendy reassured him. "I took him over to the zoo. The Animal Welfare came for him."

Otto let out a relieved sigh. "Thank you, child," he said simply. His attention returned to her suggestion. "What is 'drag'?"

"Race," she explained. "Race you back to the apartment, the side door."

"Foolish child," he chuckled and sprinted off.

"Hey! Wait for me," Wendy yelled at the disappearing figure. Never, not even at a field meet, had she seen anybody run as fast as that!

He was waiting when she arrived, leaning carelessly against the door, grinning at her astonishment. "Dear child. There are some things us bears do much, much better than humans."

Wendy couldn't argue the point. She laughed in agreement and in relief at this happy ending to all the troubles of the past few hours.

They pushed her bike into the bike room and from there let themselves into the inner lobby. Joe, probably off parking somebody's car, was nowhere around. The east elevator was at ground level, its door open, almost as though it had been expecting them.

Upstairs, the door to the apartment was flung wide with reckless unconcern. Ursula Ma'am's eyes were glistening, her smile broad. "Oh, I never"—the soft voice quavered—"I never was so happy to see you. Dear Otto."

They crowded into the foyer. Laughing, Otto and Ursula Ma'am hugged. Wendy stood nearby, warmed by their gladness.

Ursula Ma'am pulled her into the hug. "Child, you are such a good friend. A truly pleasing little human, you are."

In the depths of the furry embrace, Wendy glowed.

Otto sailed the cowboy hat like a Frisbee into the hall that led to the den. He shook his head, and his fur stood out like a halo. "Ooooff! Hate that head thing."

Smiling in self-satisfaction, he withdrew two nice-sized fish from his pockets, holding them up by the tails.

"Otto!" Ursula Ma'am clapped her paws in delight, then took the fish.

He looked smug. "Knew all the time there were fish in that there pond." He dug into an inside pocket and withdrew another. He offered it to Wendy. "Now you just taste the difference, child."

Gingerly, Wendy took the fish. It was quite stiff and, from having occupied Otto's pocket for some time, thoroughly dry. The eye stared at her, and she had to work up enthusiasm for the gift. "Gee, thanks, Otto. We—we'll eat it for dinner tonight." Which was probably going to be true. Sirloin they would not be having.

Otto let the coat drop to the floor and shook himself as though he had just come out of the water. "Don't know how humans stand all these things." He stepped to the living room door. Eyes closed, slowly, luxuriously, he scratched his back against the door frame. "Ooooo." It was a contented sound. "This is the way we're supposed to be, us bears. Just fur."

He picked up the coat and padded down the hall after the cowboy hat. "Better put away the fur hiders. Never can tell when I'll need them again."

"No," protested Ursula Ma'am. "Not to go out, Otto."

Wendy trailed after him, alarmed. "Hey, Otto. You can't do this again. You just can't. I only got us out of that jam with a lot of luck."

The telephone rang.

Ursula Ma'am gave a pleased little hop. "Dr. Corrigan. He talked to me when you were gone, child."

Wendy ran for the extension in the den.

"Wendy? Did you retrieve Otto from the park?"

There was pride in the single word of her reply. "Wait."

She thrust the phone at the dazed-looking Otto. "I forgot to tell you Dr. Corrigan called this morning. Here. Just talk in there." She tapped the mouthpiece.

Otto looked doubtfully at the telephone, brought it close to his mouth. "That you, Dr. Corrigan?" he roared.

Wendy winced and covered the mouthpiece. "You don't have to yell. Just talk, like you do to me. He'll hear."

"Uh, hello. Dr. Corrigan?" he said in more normal tones. He listened, looking pleased. "Yep." Pause. "Yep." Pause. "Got us some fine fish from that pond down there." A long pause. "Well . . . if you say so. All right. I won't then." Pause. "Yep. Right here."

Wendy took the phone.

Laughter greeted her. "You've had your hands full, I can see. I didn't expect you to get involved in this, but I have to admit I'm glad you've been there to cushion the bumps."

The bears crowded close, their heads next to hers, listening.

"I couldn't call before today," Dr. Corrigan continued. "We're working here in the mountains, you know—"

"Our mountain," whispered Ursula Ma'am.

"—and unexpected things occur at this altitude. An

early blizzard locked us in here for days. There was no way of getting to town to call."

"Seen the snows many a time," rumbled Otto.

"We're in town now to pick up provisions for the men back at camp. Then we'll pack up our specimens to send home. It'll be several days before I get there. Now tell me. Did Ursula Ma'am get the antenna assembled?"

Ursula Ma'am answered for herself. "Just like in the book."

"I knew you could do it," came the approving reply. "Wendy? Are you still there?"

"Uh-huh."

"I want you to run over to Ace Hardware and pick up a heavy-duty extension cord. Got that?"

She repeated the words.

"That's so you won't overload the circuits again. Do you have any money?"

She had spent her savings for food. But she still had something. "I've got a twenty-dollar bill my grandpa sent me for my birthday. Only I'm not supposed to spend it without clearing it with my mother."

There was a thoughtful silence. "Wendy, ordinarily I wouldn't condone going against maternal orders. But this is an emergency. Otto and Ursula Ma'am must begin sending. It's entirely possible—as we understand space flight—that the Others require that beam in order

108

to find their entry slot into our atmosphere. But above and beyond that, they need to communicate with Otto and Ursula Ma'am. I feel it's acceptable to use your money in these circumstances. I'll send you money to replace it. Be on the lookout for a letter. Now let me talk to Otto, please."

She left the bears absorbed in something Dr. Corrigan was explaining. All the way to Ace Hardware she repeated what she wanted. A heavy-duty extension cord. A heavy-duty extension cord. A heavy-duty . . .

The antenna was mounted on the radio when she got back. The businesslike affair, all angled metal rods, taller than she, was a cold and foreign thing among the big corduroy chairs and stacks of books in the comfortable room.

She strung the extension cord, as thick as her thumb, from the wall outlet to the radio, then sat back on her heels.

Ursula Ma'am stroked the burnished knots of the flute and lifted it. Otto touched the switch. The panel light glowed.

Quiet reigned. Beautiful, serene, undisturbed stillness. The three exchanged looks of satisfaction. Yes. Everything was all right.

Otto turned knobs. A needle on one of the dials swung to the center. "Now, love," he whispered.

Ursula Ma'am's music swelled through the room.

Wendy shivered. Never, not if she heard it a thousand million times, would she get used to the sheer delight of bear music.

As the flute spun strands of rippling loveliness, a change came over Ursula Ma'am. Her shyness fell away and she was cloaked in enormous dignity. She was— was— "Like a queen," Wendy thought, watching in awe.

Otto came alive to Wendy's presence. He shook himself. "It is the Sound," he whispered, his eyes still fixed on Ursula Ma'am.

Wendy inched closer.

"Not all of us can make the Sound. I cannot. But Ursula Ma'am, she learned from her sire, and he from his, and I think that long ago that Old One learned it from his dam. It is revered among us, the Sound. It is why I will always call her Ma'am." His eyes twinkled. "Except when I call her 'love'."

Wendy listened so hard she felt as though her head were floating like a balloon on a string. But listen as she might, she had to admit, "I can't understand what the music says. But oh, I do love it so."

Otto nodded wisely. "That is as it should be. No human should understand. Only bears."

After a time Ursula Ma'am lowered her flute. She blinked, shook her head. Her eyes focused on Wendy.

Otto flicked the off switch. "We will send many messages now. The Others will hear, and then they will speak to us."

"Dr. Corrigan," murmured Ursula Ma'am, "he said to send them at different times so humans will not guess when they are to happen."

"Why?" Wendy wanted to know. "If humans can't understand the messages, what difference does it make if they hear? They might *like* the music."

Otto wasn't sure. "Dr. Corrigan told us that many times. I think . . . I think humans can catch us if they know when the messages will happen."

Wendy's mood flattened. Otto and Ursula Ma'am were in danger from so many directions. From the hunters. From old Mrs. Constable. From Hans and Felix. And now from thousands of humans who might hear the music on their radios.

Otto coiled the cord near the radio. But there was no point in pushing it behind the draperies, not with the antenna. That they could not hide. They would simply have to leave it out and hope Hans and Felix didn't come into the apartment.

The rest of that unforgettable day was quietly satisfying, filled with golden music and the cheerings.

Bits and pieces of the mountain flowed seemingly without end from the valise. Wendy loved touching them and hearing stories about them and trying to identify them without looking at Dr. Corrigan's printed labels.

Each chip of bark was from a tree, and she knew the names of those trees. She was learning the name of each pebble and rock, too, from the "R" volume of the encyclopedia, which Miss Bunchley had not missed. Quartz, obsidian, mica were some of them. The flowers in the book were the most fun, though. She knew the dogtooth violet, the trillium, the columbine, the bitterroot. Only she kept mixing up the sugarbowl and the pasqueflower, which she pronounced pas-cue-flower. As for the hard scientific names—well, she would never learn those in nine million years!

At four o'clock, Mrs. Tulippe time, she ran downstairs humming, imagining how the tune would sound if Ursula Ma'am played it. She felt quietly hopeful, now that Ursula Ma'am and Otto had a radio that worked.

She let herself into the kitchen. She would just drop off her math book and go out the front entrance and down the hall for gingersnaps and milk from the blue glass mug, as she did each day. And then there would be at least another whole hour to spend upstairs before her mother got home from work.

Running footsteps sounded in the hall. Her mother appeared in the kitchen door, her face chalky. "Wendy! Where in the world have you been all day? I've been frantic with worry!"

Chapter 12

It was awful. As awful as anything could possibly be.

"Wendy." Her mother's eyes were red. She had been crying! The thought increased Wendy's wretchedness. "I want to know where you've been and why you didn't go to school today."

What was she to say? She had given her word and crossed her heart that very first day that she wouldn't tell about Otto and Ursula Ma'am. She licked her dry lips. Miserably, she told bits of the truth. "It was such a—a nice day. And I rode my bike in the park. And maybe it's the very last nice day before it gets really cold, and . . ."

"And you played with a strange dog," her mother said levelly.

Oh no! How did her mother know about the black-and-tan dog? What else did she know?

Wendy studied her knuckles, realized they were grubby, and hastily hid her hand behind her back before her mother found something more to be upset about. "Well, there weren't any kids around. And it was kind of lonesome."

The wrong thing to say. Definitely the wrong thing.

"You didn't have to be lonesome. Not with Kelly and Sara and all your friends at school." The last word was pointed.

With her toe, Wendy traced the design of one of the floor tiles.

Her mother sighed and led the way to the living room. Wendy followed, feet dragging. Her mother sank onto the sofa. Wendy leaned against the desk. She picked up a paperweight. A piece of amber with a fly in it was embedded in the glass. The fly was about a thousand years old. It had got trapped in the amber. She felt trapped too.

"Wendy, how often have you done this?"

Oh my gosh! Did her mother think she was some kind of delinquent? "But I never did!" Wendy protested.

Her mother didn't speak, just looked at her. Then she said, "Well, I'm glad at least for that."

But how had her mother known about the dog? The policeman—

Almost as if in answer to the question, her mother spoke. "Mr. McDonough called me. A police officer stopped at school and told him some story about finding you in the park with a dog. What was that all about?"

Wendy squirmed. That's all her mother knew, then. She didn't know about Otto and Ursula Ma'am. And

Wendy wouldn't tell, either. Not if they tortured her and tied her up and made her eat cream cheese for a thousand years. "It was just some dog. I fed it. That's all." Only it wasn't all. Wait until her mother found out about the sirloin. Oh misery!

Her mother eyed her for a moment. "All right, Wendy. I suppose everyone has to try cutting school once in a lifetime. But now that you've had this burst of preadolescent independence, you are to stick to the rules."

She talked on. Endlessly. About how well the two of them got along. About how that was because they trusted each other and did their "jobs." About how could she go out of town on business not knowing if Wendy would behave herself.

Wendy turned the paperweight and watched the light change in it. Suddenly there were two pieces of amber, two flies. And she felt awful, with a deep sickness that reached right down to her toes. Because she hadn't meant to make her mother cry. She hadn't thought about her mother at all.

"—want to punish you." Her mother's voice jarred Wendy out of her thoughts. "But I'm going to have to, to make you understand."

Wendy was alert.

"No telephone. No playing with Kelly and Sara for the next week."

Ha! As if they wanted to play with her!

"You're to come straight home from school and stay with Mrs. Tulippe until I get in from work."

How can I help Otto and Ursula Ma'am, Wendy wailed inwardly, *if I have to stay locked up with Mrs. Tee?*

"Now you go to your room while I do some work I brought home from the office. And start your memorizing."

Memorizing. That was part of punishment in the Devlin household. Once she had lost one of a new pair of shoes, and that meant twenty-five lines. A fib about not eating the whole bottom layer of a box of candy—except the four corner pieces—had meant forty lines.

"Four pages," said her mother calmly.

"Four!" moaned Wendy. "I'll forget the beginning before I get to the end."

The sentence was firm. "Actors do it all the time. Four."

Dragging her feet, thinking bleak thoughts of prisoners and dungeons, Wendy went to her room. She kicked off her shoes and curled up on her bed with *Alice in Wonderland.* Daddy had liked to read to her from *Alice.* He hadn't just read, actually. Every one of the characters, the March Hare, or the Queen, or the Cheshire Cat, had a special way of talking. Reading with Daddy had been like being at a play. For a moment, remembering, she felt comforted.

It was unfair! Downright unfair! She had only wanted to help Otto and Ursula Ma'am. If her mother knew about them, she would want to help too.

She remembered the hurt, disappointed look in her mother's eyes and cried for a while. Only that didn't help much. So she blew her nose and opened her book, considering the awesome possibility that before she grew up she might have memorized the whole of *Alice in Wonderland*.

The apartment was unnaturally quiet. In the silence, the elevator doors could be heard faintly, opening and closing. The afternoon paper hit the door with a *thunk*. The clock in the hall chimed the quarter hours.

After a time her mother started moving around. Hollow clanks and clatters came from the kitchen.

Footsteps approached her door. "Wendy? What happened to the sirloin I was planning for dinner? And where did that fish in the refrigerator come from?"

Wendy's ears reddened. "I fed it to the dog," she mumbled into the pages of her book.

"You what?" Her mother's voice slid up the scale. "That just doesn't make sense!" She considered. "But then none of your behavior today makes sense. And the fish?"

"Otto gave it to me." The words slipped out before Wendy realized it.

"Otto? You haven't mentioned him before. A new boy in your class?"

Wendy nodded, not looking up.

"Well, we'll have the fish for dinner, then." Her mother started to leave, turned back. "Maybe Otto doesn't know that polite fishermen clean and scale their catch. You might tactfully tell him that." She made a face. "I do hate scaling fish!"

The days that followed were faintly unreal. Wendy felt as though she were living somebody else's life.

Even before class began next morning, Miss Bunchley sent her to the office to see Mr. McDonough. Kelly's and Sara's eyes bored into her back as she left the room.

Mr. McDonough's face was lined and kind, under a thatch of snowy hair that took on a pink cast from his very rosy scalp. Wendy had never seen anything but a jolly Mr. McDonough. But he was stern this morning. "Come in, Wendy."

She advanced to his desk feeling as though she were put together with bolts that were too tight. She and Kelly and Sara had often wondered what happened to kids who were sent to Mr. McDonough. Now she was finding out.

"Wendy, you know we just can't stay away from school anytime we like." He went on to talk about her "job"—that again. And about there being rules for everybody—which just wasn't true because grown-ups didn't have rules. He finished by saying, "You haven't done this before, and so I'm not going to punish you. But I am going to ask for your word that it won't happen again."

He waited, his eyes fixed on her.

How could she promise that? Biting her lip, she considered the dilemma. If something happened to Otto and Ursula Ma'am, she would just have to help, even if it meant staying away from school.

"Wendy?"

She wasn't going to get out of this office unless she promised. She had to say it, even if it wasn't going to be true. "I won't."

Mr. McDonough came around the desk. He spoke kindly. "Wendy, sometimes when we're growing up our problems are too big to handle. It helps to talk about them. Will you remember that if you want to talk about anything, the door to this office is always open?"

Wendy studied her shoes. Her head bobbed.

He patted her head. "All right then. Run along now."

He didn't really mean "run," but Wendy did, banging the door on the way out. In the hall, she leaned against the drinking fountain. Her mouth felt like a desert, and her heart was thumping away as though she had just run a hundred miles.

Miss Bunchley was passing out math papers as

Wendy slid into her seat.

Sara smiled shyly, her upper lip curled down over her braces. "Was it bad, Wendy?" she asked sympathetically.

"Uh-uh." Wendy whispered back. "He only talks a lot."

Kelly swung around in her seat. "My gosh, Wendy! What'd you pull?" There were equal measures of admiration and curiosity in the question.

Miss Bunchley started talking about metrics.

"Tell you later," Wendy whispered.

Her cheek resting on her hand, she listened half-heartedly. She couldn't tell Kelly and Sara about Otto and Ursula Ma'am until after the bears had gone. But, oh, she was glad they were making up, glad to have her friends back.

There wasn't time to talk during the morning. Wendy went to accelerated reading, and Kelly to special help math, and Sara had a singing lesson. But they sat together at lunch and it was just like old times.

Kelly lined up a row of caramels around her plate for the Big Dessert after her regular dessert. Sara eyed them longingly, running the tip of her tongue along her braces.

Kelly had half of her grilled-cheese sandwich eaten before Wendy had taken so much as a single bite of her hot dog. "We're going to my house to watch TV this after—" she said, talking around the sandwich. "Want to come?"

Wendy told the truth. "I can't go anywhere except straight home for a whole week. And I can't use the phone or go to your houses or ask you to come to mine."

Kelly stopped in mid-bite. "My gosh, Wendy. You must have put poison in your mother's tea at least."

Sara thought she understood everything about the last week. "You've been grounded! And that's why you didn't come with us last week! That's it!"

Kelly's grilled-cheese sandwich lay on her plate, turning to cardboard. "Wendy Devlin, what . . . did . . . you . . . do?"

"I gave my word not to tell," Wendy said vaguely. "Only I'll tell you when it's all over."

Kelly prodded relentlessly. "When's that?"

"Soon, I guess." Wendy bit into her hot dog.

Sara, always sympathetic, said, "You're practically a prisoner."

Wendy's very thought. "Like the Count of Monte Cristo," she agreed.

"Bread and water," breathed Kelly, touched to the core of her greedy heart.

Wendy softened the pathetic picture. "Well, and chicken soup." Then, unwilling to give up entirely on herself as prisoner, she added, "And—and gruel.

Thin." She had read that in *Oliver Twist*. "With lumps in it," she added forlornly.

Kindhearted Sara would bring cookies and fruit to Wendy for the rest of the week.

After school, before reporting to Mrs. Tulippe, Wendy slipped upstairs for a few minutes. Otto and Ursula Ma'am listened with concern to her tale of troubles.

"Poor child," Otto rumbled. "We brought this on you."

"Well, I don't care," Wendy said firmly. "I want to help you." She poked at the bridge of her glasses. "Did you hear anything? Did the Others answer yet?"

They hadn't, but Ursula Ma'am was confident. "It's not to fret, child. We will hear. We will."

Her hand on the doorknob, ready to run downstairs to take up her imprisonment, Wendy remembered something else. "My mom's string group is coming tonight."

The bears looked puzzled.

"They play music," she explained, adding, "Human music's nice too."

"The windows are open." Otto pointed. "Maybe we will hear it."

"What kind of story does human music tell?" Ursula Ma'am asked brightly.

Wendy couldn't say. Was there a story? If there was, she had never picked it out of the music. Maybe

Otto and Ursula Ma'am could tell her the story. If there was one.

Wendy loved her mother's string group nights. It was so special to have "live" music right there in her very own living room. She liked the people who played it, most of whom she had known all her life. And she got to stay up an extra hour, besides. Or, usually she did.

Tonight she waited for her mother to say that people who were being punished had to stay in their rooms. But her mother said nothing. Maybe she thought Wendy was suffering enough, not being able to see Kelly and Sara. Or maybe she thought music was good for Wendy. At any rate, when the night doorman buzzed from the lobby to let them know guests were on their way up, Wendy held the door open, waiting, as she always did. Chad Clement and Felicia Simon got off the elevator in a flurry of laughter. Wendy closed the door after them and took their coats.

The living room overflowed with talk and activity. Chairs were set in a circle. Collapsible music stands sprouted. Velvet-lined instrument cases were opened. Quietly, Wendy raised the corner window directly below the open one upstairs.

The harsh buzz of the intercom announced another arrival.

"Oh," exclaimed Mrs. Devlin. "Rob couldn't make

it tonight. I asked Peter Quirk—I've mentioned him —to sit in. That will be him."

A grayness of spirit descended on Wendy. Why hadn't her mother warned her? She stamped to the door, scowling.

Mr. Quirk got off the elevator, smiling broadly, cradling a violin case. "Hello, chum," he said, ruffling her hair in passing.

Wendy ducked out from beneath his hand. *I do not like you to touch my hair*, she said silently, and closed the door behind him more forcefully than was necessary. She trailed after him into the living room.

There was more talk and laughter.

"How nice." That was Felicia to Mr. Ugh. "Barbara says you played with a group in Columbus."

"We can use another violin," Chad said heartily.

Mr. Quirk's tie and shirt and socks were all a highly visible lime green. And yes, "it" was there, stuck into his tie. Nobody seemed to notice.

Look at that terrible horrible eyeball, Wendy yelled mutely. Why were grown-ups so dense? *I'll never understand them*, she thought. *Never. Not in a billion years.*

Bows were rosined, pages of music turned, instruments tuned with raw little scrapings and pluckings. The room was hushed for an expectant moment, and then the group swept into a romping piece of music Wendy especially liked.

Curled in a corner of the sofa, she dusted her cheek with the brush end of her queue and forgot about punishments. The music darted and flowed around her, enclosing her in a sparkling web of song.

Suddenly a sound of such sweetness lifted above the music that Wendy caught her breath. A surprised look passed among the musicians. Instantly her mother's cello and the viola and violin softened to an accompaniment. Mr. Quirk's eyes were closed, his face above the lime green shirt composed. And the silvery tones poured from his violin.

Confused, unbelieving, Wendy watched him. Mr. Quirk of the weird eyeballs. Mr. Quirk of the frightful ties and go-along socks. Mr. Quirk of "Hello, chum," and insultingly easy puzzles—*that* Mr. Quirk could make music like this. . . .

The haunting strain softened. The accompaniment rose in volume to enclose it.

Unmoving, Wendy listened to the end, heard Chad and Felicia speak warmly of Mr. Quirk's "interpretation," saw her mother's quiet glow.

Lying in bed later, the music drifting into her room, Wendy tried to sort out her feelings.

Never had she heard such music. Never, at least, from a human. Bear music was incredibly beautiful. But it wasn't fair to count bear music. She had to compare Mr. Ugh's music to other human music. Doing so, she had to admit she loved it. Only, she didn't love the maker of the music.

How could she like Mr. Quirk's music and not like Mr. Quirk? Even now she could pick out the sound of his violin from among the other instruments.

She slid out of bed and closed her door.

The music, though softened, crept in anyway.

She pulled the blue comforter over her head. And the music kept right on going, inside her head.

When she slept at last, she dreamed of being lost in a forest of rainbow-colored trees. One of the trees had a knot in it. She looked closer, and in the knot was an eyeball. It winked at her.

Chapter 13

Wendy could only spend minutes with Otto and Ursula Ma'am the next afternoon before reporting to Mrs. Tulippe. The bears were excited about the music of the night before.

"I never knew humans had anything so beautiful to" —Ursula Ma'am groped for words, finally fell back on her own experience—"to cheer them."

Otto paid the music his highest compliment. "Very bearish. Even if we could not understand the story," he added.

"You couldn't?" Wendy was disappointed. "Isn't there a story?" She had so wanted there to be!

Ursula Ma'am tried to ease her disappointment. "Maybe there is, only we could not hear it."

Otto tried to explain. "It's like we can't understand the foxes and deer, or them us. Foxes talk to foxes and deer to deer. And bears to each other. It's like it's all meant for a secret, each for its own kind."

Wendy's forehead wrinkled. "But you talk to *me*."

"And isn't that cheerful!" Ursula Ma'am's soft voice

caressed the word. "Who's to explain how it happens to be?" She shook her head to clear it of such perplexing ideas and returned to the music. "No, we could not understand your story. But the music talked, all the same."

"It did?"

"It talked about the humans who made it," said Ursula Ma'am. "The deep flowing, like underground rivers of—of—honey." She emitted a sound that was startlingly cello-like. "The human who did that—"

Wendy was attentive. She was going to hear something interesting about her mother.

"That human is strong and gentle and understands more than words. But that human yearns."

Yearn. That meant to want something. What could her mother be wanting?

Otto spoke. "The high sweetness—"

That could only be Mr. Quirk.

"That human has"—he searched for words—"has . . . sweetness of spirit . . ."

Mr. Quirk? *Sweet?*

". . . but he walks within a shadow of his own making."

Wendy had never seen any shadows around Mr. Quirk. The neon colors of his ties and socks lit up any room he entered.

Otto stared out at the sun-gilded top of a nearby building. "That human seeks understanding and friendship." He turned back to Wendy. "His music says he does not find it."

Wendy had nothing to say. She had never thought of Mr. Quirk as anything but—but what? Certainly not *sweet!*

The bears were getting ready to start sending as she left. She wanted most desperately to stay. But she dared not. Mrs. Tulippe knew she had to be there by four.

She's my jailkeeper, Wendy thought glumly, stamping downstairs, passing through the Devlin apartment and out into the hall. She tapped on the door at the other end of the corridor.

The rattle of locks did little to erase the idea of jails from her mind, although Mrs. Tulippe's distressed murmurs as she struggled with them were hardly jailer-like. "Dear me. Mercy. Oh, mercy."

Watching a funny old movie about a kid called Andy Hardy, Wendy let her mind drift. Yes, she guessed Mr. Quirk looked for friendship. And no, he did not find it. At least not from her. She tried to put together the pieces of the puzzle that was Mr. Quirk. Incredible ties. Go-along socks. Eyeball tie tacks. Soaring music. And shadows. You could make a shadow, all right. Everyone did. But how could you stand in it?

She sighed. This much she did know: colors were grayed in shadow. She knew that from art class.

"Dear, dear, dear," chirruped Mrs. Tulippe, "but

don't we look gloomy. Now dear, let's just get you another prune chewy and some more milk."

Dispiritedly Wendy followed her toward the kitchen. Behind her, the sound from the TV erupted into a discordant crackle.

Wendy spun around.

The picture was flopping wildly. Then it broke up into a crazy pattern of squiggles and dancing dots.

Mrs. Tulippe wrung her hands. "It's going to explode."

Wendy dived for the off switch. *Neat*, she thought. *Now I'm not only locked up in here after school, but there's no TV*. Things could not, could *not*, get any worse.

Mrs. Tulippe seemed to remember that she was the grown-up and was supposed to be in charge in emergencies. "I'll have Hans look at it tomorrow," she said in calmer tones. "Now let's just get you your cookies. And then," she added brightly, "we can look at my photograph album. There are lots of pictures of my Theresa when she was your age."

The rest of the afternoon was spent with old Theresa. Theresa in a pony cart. Theresa in a scout uniform. Theresa in a band outfit.

Wendy had seen Theresa once. She was a fat lady who wore false eyelashes so long you could hardly see her eyes through them. It was hard to believe she had once been the girl in the pictures, and harder still to believe the girl could have been anything at all like kids today.

The letter from Dr. Corrigan came the next day. It was in the mailbox when Wendy got home from school, addressed to her in the unmistakable beautiful printing Dr. Corrigan used instead of writing. She opened it on the way upstairs.

"Well, hello Wendy, my human friend," the letter began. Now wasn't that just like Dr. Corrigan? Other people started letters "Dear" someone or other. Not Dr. Corrigan.

Enclosed is twenty dollars to replace the money you used to buy the extension cord. There's also something extra here to buy more food. Otto told me about the food and the "waterfall." That was kind and thoughtful of you.

Even though I didn't intend you to get involved in this, I'm pleased you're getting to know Otto and Ursula Ma'am. They are unique bears, and their ideals are truly remarkable.

I expect to be back in town in just a few days, and then I'll take over on things. Until then, many thanks for helping.

Your friend,
W. C. Corrigan

P.S. I think it would be a good idea to buy more fish. Otto especially likes trout.

Wendy grinned. And it would help to keep Otto out of the park. Dr. Corrigan didn't say that, but he meant it all the same.

She took twenty dollars out of the envelope to put back into Grandpa's letter. She tucked the rest of the money into her math book for shopping on her way home from school.

There was a good deal of thinking time that week, after school at Mrs. Tulippe's and evenings without the phone, and there was more than a little to think about.

Otto and Ursula Ma'am didn't hear from the Others, but they weren't worried and their confidence was catching. The Others were coming, without any doubt. When wasn't known. How wasn't known. But come they would. And then Otto and Ursula Ma'am would no longer have to worry about being fenced in on the mountain. They would just go away, and—

It was here Wendy's thoughts always stopped. "Going away" meant "forever." She had not yet faced that fact.

She had other things to think about too.

Her mother was "yearning" for something. Wendy could not imagine what that might be. Knowing that her mother was troubled set Wendy's world atilt.

And then there was Mr. Quirk. Thoughts of the brilliantly hued Mr. Quirk continued to make Wendy deeply unhappy. Her mother liked him. Otto and Ursula Ma'am did too—or, at least they liked his music.

His music. At unexpected moments, when she wasn't thinking anything in particular, the remembered sounds of his violin echoed in her head.

Why didn't Mr. Quirk just go away and not come back?

He came and went several times that week. Wendy, thinking of "shadows" and "seeking friendship" and his music, permitted herself to be patted on the head. She laughed politely at corny jokes and, without being told, said thank you for a ladybug magnet. Her mother looked at her penetratingly but did not comment.

Her mother was nicer than usual, that long week. She didn't poke around in Wendy's mind with all sorts of questions, as some grown-ups might have. She just seemed to want to be near Wendy. She even read aloud to her one evening, something she hadn't done since Wendy learned to read by herself. They both enjoyed that.

Friday, Kelly and Sara talked excitedly about sleeping that night at Kelly's. "I wish you could come, too, Wendy," said Kelly. Her eyes danced. "My parents are going to an alderman's coffee hour in our building. We can play the stereo as loud as we want while they're gone."

"It would be lots more fun if you could come, Wendy." Sara offered her a wrinkled brown bag. "There's a banana and Oreos and some caramels in here."

Wendy took the bag, feeling guilty. Not about the fib, but because she had forgotten what a believing nature Sara had. Sara needed someone to look after her so people wouldn't take advantage of her. Wendy vowed to be that someone, after Otto and Ursula Ma'am left. She gave Sara a quick hug.

That night as Wendy was getting ready for bed, her mother came into her room. For a long moment she watched her brushing the tangles out of her hair, then took the brush out of her hand. "Let me."

She brushed with long, smooth strokes that tugged Wendy's head to one side. Her eyes met Wendy's in the mirror and she paused. "Look. You're nearly up to my shoulder. You've grown such a lot in the last year Daddy would hardly know you."

Wendy bit her lip. It all seemed such a long time ago, when Daddy was with them.

Her mother patted her cheek and went on with the brushing. She arranged Wendy's hair around her shoulders and smiled at her. "It would be so pretty like this. Like Alice in Wonderland. Daddy would say you're about ready to go into a new phase."

Talking about growing up and new phases was hard enough. But it was bringing Daddy into it that did it. Wendy's throat felt stiff and as though tears were running down inside.

"I don't want to look like Alice in Wonderland," she blurted out. "I want to look like me. Like I looked when Daddy was here. I don't want to change." Her voice quivered. "Not ever."

"So that's what's in your mind these days." Her mother's words were soft. She sank down on the bed and pulled Wendy, big as she was, onto her lap. She rocked gently and smoothed her hair.

Wendy cried, quietly, wetly, all over her mother's dress.

After a while her mother began to talk. "Tippy, growing up is just going through one phase after another. Daddy got a real kick out of all your phases.

"When you first insisted on feeding yourself, we had to put up with spinach in your hair and beet finger paintings on the wall."

Wendy gave a hiccupy giggle.

"Daddy laughed—he didn't have to clean up the mess—and said it was a sign of healthy creativity. And when you got your first tricycle—"

"It was blue," Wendy mumbled, listening hard.

"We were out for a walk one day and Daddy tried to help you up a curb, and you said, 'I can do it by myself.' Daddy was pleased and said you weren't a baby anymore, but he thought he was going to like having a little person around the house. That was another phase.

"When you started school, you didn't want us to walk you there after the first few weeks. Daddy wasn't surprised. He said you were independent and he was glad, and he took you down to the corner to show you the walk signal."

"That's the first word I learned to print," said Wendy, highly interested in this chronicle of her growing up. "He said I could go by myself when I could print it. I learned that very day."

"Since then you've gone through lots more phases—"

"Like when I drew pictures on his music?"

"Thank heavens you outgrew that one pretty fast."

"He spanked me," Wendy recalled.

"Only after you'd been warned several times. And it did seem to nudge you out of that phase. But what I'm trying to say is, Daddy watched you go through all kinds of growing-up stages and he loved you in them all. If he could see you now, he'd say, 'She's growing up fast. Next thing you know it'll be the boys.'"

"Never," muttered Wendy.

Her mother laughed in that infuriating I-know-better way of grown-ups.

"Wendy, looks don't count a whole lot. Hair in pigtails or a queue or hanging loose—it doesn't really matter. The person is still you. Daddy would like you however you fixed your hair, or dressed, or grew."

A pleasing sense of the rightness of things settled over Wendy. She fingered the silky fall of her hair around her face. It did feel nice and swingy, all hanging loose.

Chapter 14

Wendy lounged in the kitchen doorway, watching her mother scrape something into a baking dish. Her mother was dressed for work but had a big towel wrapped around her middle to protect her dress. It was the next morning. Saturday.

"What's that?"

"Your 'most favorite' dessert, pineapple divinity."

Wendy's mouth watered. "Yummmm."

Her mother slid the dish into the oven. "I thought we needed a treat this weekend." She began cleaning up the cooking mess.

Wendy had a favor to ask.

"Mom, I'll trade you twofors—two Saturdays for one—if you'll only let me have this one Saturday off my sentence." It mattered desperately. She just had to spend today upstairs with Otto and Ursula Ma'am.

For some reason her mother's lips twitched. "Well-ll—"

"Please-please-please," Wendy pleaded. She came into the kitchen and leaned against the counter, doing her best to look wan. "I'll get weak and pale if I don't get sunshine. After a while I won't be able to see, like those fish that live in caves."

Her mother laughed. She studied Wendy's face. "Life's been difficult lately, hasn't it, Tippy?" She ran water in the sink. "All right, then. We'll relax the rules this once."

Wendy let out a whoop and threw her arms around her mother. "Mom, you're just the neatest human!"

Her mother's eyebrows lifted. "What a peculiar choice of words."

Wendy felt her cheeks warm. She had slipped again. She gave her mother an extra squeeze and turned to leave. Her eyes fell on a crumpled silvery wrapping on the counter. "What's that?" she asked suspiciously.

"The wrapper from the cream cheese," her mother said calmly.

"But what's it doing here?" Wendy knew. Even before her mother said it, she knew.

"I needed it for the pineapple divinity," her mother said calmly.

"That's mean," Wendy yelped. "You knew that's my most favorite dessert, and you went and put cream cheese in it, and you know I hate cream cheese."

"But darling, cream cheese is one of the basic ingredients in pineapple divinity. It always has been. You've been eating cream cheese in pineapple divinity for years."

Wendy felt betrayed. Her very own mother had been

138

feeding her cream cheese! How could she!

Her mother dried her hands and reached out to adjust Wendy's glasses. "Honestly, how do you see!" Then, comfortingly, she continued, "All kinds of things get baked together and you can't even tell they're there. You just wait and see. You won't even taste the cream cheese. Your 'most favorite' dessert will be the same as ever.

"Now you run along and enjoy this day off your 'sentence'. Mrs. Tulippe expects you for lunch. I'll be home from the office by three and I'll expect you here then."

In her room, Wendy sat on her bed to put on her shoes, wondering if she was ever going to like pine-apple divinity again, knowing there was cream cheese in it. It would be a terrible loss.

Straightening, she read the note on her bedside table. She had stayed awake a long time last night, thinking about her father, about changing, about growing and what that meant.

Her mother's words about phases and about changes not mattering because you were still the same person got mixed up somehow with other words about rocks changing and mountains groaning and pine needles being loved no matter what happened to them. She just couldn't sort it all out. It might take a long time. She might be thirteen or fourteen before she even began to understand.

And there was more besides. It was part of the growing-up thing, in some shadowy way. If you were growing up, you had to do things now and then that didn't exactly please you. Like going to the dentist and not making a fuss. Like being polite about presents you really didn't like.

Pushing at her glasses with a forefinger, she reread the note.

Dear Mom,
It's okay to marry Mr. Quirk if you want to. The way he plays the violin is really something.

Love,
Wendy

Impulsively she added a P.S.

I guess a person could get used to go-along socks and eyeballs and all that if they really tried.

She underlined *tried* three times and drew round eyes and a smiling mouth in the "O" of Love. Then before she could change her mind, she folded the note and pushed it into her shirt pocket.

Passing her desk, she opened her math book and withdrew Dr. Corrigan's money. Food was getting low upstairs. She folded the bills and tucked them securely away in her deepest pocket.

She listened in the hall. From where she stood, she

could see her mother's briefcase on the desk in the living room. The sound of pillows being fluffed came from her mother's room. She had to be quick.

Inside the case were a handful of sharp pencils and a bunchy set of folded galley proofs. She paperclipped her note to the first page where it couldn't be missed.

An ache gnawed at her middle. Her hand seemed to have a will of its own—it wanted to stick to the note. What she was doing was so final. Still . . . She thought again of the talk she had had with her mother last night. Growing up meant more than just letting your hair fall free. She closed the briefcase with a firm, soft click.

There.

She didn't call good-bye, but let herself quietly out into the service hallway.

Upstairs, she had to wait longer than usual. Otto opened the door at last, his paw at his lips. Hurriedly she stepped inside.

Music came from the front of the apartment. But it wasn't Ursula Ma'am's music. Wendy's scalp prickled. She tiptoed down the hall and into the living room as if she were entering some forbidden temple.

Ursula Ma'am was on the floor, her flute untouched beside her, listening intently to the curious sounds that welled from the radio. Otto settled down beside her, Wendy's presence forgotten, his lips silently forming the words he heard in the music.

Wendy sank down beside them, cross-legged, searching their faces for an understanding of what was happening.

The music! Listening, Wendy hugged herself. Played
to a scale no human had ever heard or even thought
of, made by instruments she could not imagine—oh,
could even the world's greatest musician dream of such
music? Without increasing in volume, curiously, it
swelled and soared, larger somehow than the room,
more vast than the earth. At last it drifted to a mur-
mur . . . a whisper . . . a sigh . . . and stopped.

Ursula Ma'am's flute sent its rippling message out
into space, then, to question the unseen friends. Their
reply came in a rush. The two "voices" spoke, excited
at one moment, serene the next. They even seemed to
laugh and tease. Exactly, Wendy thought in wonder-
ment, the way humans talk to each other.

She couldn't have said for how long the strange conversation continued, or when it stopped. She knew only
that suddenly there was silence. She shook herself,
bearlike without knowing, and spoke. "Ohhhhh."

Otto switched off the radio and the bears hugged,
laughing.

Wendy looked from one to the other. What was happening? Would somebody please tell her what was
going on? She flounced impatiently.

Ursula Ma'am remembered her. "The Others are

142

coming. Oh, they are coming. They were only waiting for us to tell them where we are."

Wendy's heart pounded. Again she had that fearful sense of the world changing. "When?" she asked breathlessly. "When are they coming?"

Otto replied. "When the sun has gone to rest four times, they will come for us."

Wendy counted. Today was Saturday. . . .

"They said," he continued, "we must go up to the—"

"But that's Tuesday!" The words exploded from Wendy. "Do you really mean they're coming for you Tuesday?"

"We will be free," breathed Ursula Ma'am. "Free." She lingered on the beautiful word.

Wendy stared at Otto and Ursula Ma'am. They were going away. They really were. Forever. She would never see them again.

The largest pine cone lay on the carpet nearby. She reached for it, cradled it, fingering the lovely thing, waiting for it to cheer her, if it would.

Otto didn't allow time for cheer to set in. Plans must be made. "They said we must go up to the top of this place. Can we go there?"

It was a practical thing to think about. It took Wendy's mind away from her sad thoughts.

The roof was something she knew about. She knew about it in spite of her mother. On her mother's "fuss list" were the lobby ("Don't loiter"), her key ("Don't lose it"), and the roof deck ("I don't want you up there when it's empty").

"The elevators go up to the party room," she explained, "and the sun deck's right outside the door. Stairs go up there too."

"They will come for us there," said Otto.

"But how?"

He didn't know. But if the Others said they would come, come they would.

"Where are they now?" Endless questions wanted answers.

Ursula Ma'am gestured vaguely upward and outward. "They are waiting out there."

It gave Wendy an eerie feeling to think that somewhere near the earth a spaceship was hovering, and she was the only human who knew about it.

Another question.

"Suppose they go to the wrong building. There are lots and lots of tall buildings in the city."

"They won't." Otto was sure. "I don't know how that is, but they won't. Maybe," he added, "they know ways humans don't know.

Were there things humans—even the smartest humans in the whole world—didn't know that bears knew? That unsettling idea took its place among the many other strange ideas of this morning. They were all things to ponder on, but later.

Wendy left to shop for food, an errand to be done as quickly as possible so she wouldn't miss the next conversation with the Others.

She trudged to the Shop and Save with the empty shopping cart trundling behind her and bought every good thing she could find. Lots of fresh trout. Out-of-season berries. Juice. Peanut butter. Jelly. And she didn't have to add up as she went along or worry about whether she could pay for it at the checkout counter.

The lobby was empty when she got back—Joe was probably off parking someone's car—and she had to struggle with the heavy glass door. With a scrape and a clatter she pulled the shopping cart through and the door swung shut behind her. In the sudden quiet, voices came clearly from the manager's office just off the lobby.

". . . reCEPtion is SIMply DREADful." Mr. Pick. Only Mr. Pick talked that way.

Mrs. Jurgen's voice was soothing. ". . . complaints. Hans looked at the master antenna and found nothing wrong."

"Well, beLIEVE me, SOMEthing IS wrong."

"Next week he'll check the leads in all the apartments. Perhaps there's a break somewhere."

Mr. Pick was really having a fit. "Well, I susPECT there's MORE to it than THAT. ODD MUSIC interrupted my FM this morning too. I believe there is unAUTHorized BROADcasting in this neighborhood. If it conTINues, I FULLY intend to rePORT it to—"

Wendy's knuckles whitened on the handle of the shopping cart. She leaned forward.

A voice came from behind her. "Well now, someone's helping her mama again. That's just real nice."

Joe had returned. He bustled across the lobby and unlocked the inner door. Reluctantly she went on through it.

Misery! If only Joe had held off for a few minutes she would have heard who Mr. Pick was going to report the "unAUTHorized" broadcasting to. She had heard enough, though, to be scared.

The situation was serious. She reported what she had heard to Otto and Ursula Ma'am, and they talked about what they would do.

Early Monday they would take down the antenna. They would take apart the radio and put it back into the suitcases. Then they would wait in the den, close to the closet, ready to hide.

The rest of the morning they ate berries and peanut-butter sandwiches. From time to time, Ursula Ma'am played her flute and they listened to the reply of the Others. Otto and Ursula Ma'am nodded to each other in understanding of all they heard, and they seemed content.

Wendy listened to it all too. But instead of content-ment, she felt bleakness. And then she reached into the valise.

The cheerings didn't "cheer" Wendy as they did the bears. No. But they did something else.

She cupped a rock in her hands. It grew warm. Its roughness left its mark on her skin. The power of the mountain seemed to flow into her hands. She didn't have to look at the rock. Its color didn't matter. Only its rock-ness. And the same was true of a piece of bark, of a handful of pine needles, of a pine cone. All spoke to her. About the rightness of things of the earth, about beauty and happiness, and even about hurt. The hurt spoke in its own way. It's all part of the pattern, it seemed to say. Grow, Wendy. Grow. Be a part of it all.

She fondled the cheerings. Oh, the mountain had to be the most beautiful place in the whole world. How could Otto and Ursula Ma'am leave it? How could they? Forever?

Chapter 15

True to her word, Wendy was downstairs before three that afternoon. She was sprawled on the floor of her room, working on the double-faced jigsaw puzzle, when her mother got in from work. She came into the room, stepped over Wendy, pushed aside a clutter of stuffed animals on the low bookcase, and perched there. She leaned forward, hands gripping the edge, and just looked at Wendy. Her smile was glowing. Oddly, there were also tears in her eyes. How did grown-ups do that, laugh and cry at the same time?

"Tippy, I found your note."

Wendy spotted a piece of blue with part of a church spire that belonged in the upper right corner of the puzzle. She poked it into place, not speaking. It was just too hard to talk about some things.

"And I want to know why you wrote it."

Startled, Wendy forgot the puzzle. Why would she write it except to tell her mother exactly what it said! "Well, because I guess you want to marry Mr. Quirk and you think you can't because I don't like go-along

148

socks and stuff. Only, you can. Because—well, because I don't want you to yearn."

Her mother studied her face. "That's a very grown-up and generous thought, Tippy." It was quiet in the room. "Thank you." Then, "But do I have to marry Peter Quirk?"

Wendy's head swam. Her jaw drooped. "What?"

Her mother laughed. "Darling, I don't know that I want to marry Peter or anyone just now."

"But you—you—go out to dinner with him and he likes music and you do too, and I thought, well I thought you wanted to marry him." Isn't that what grown-ups did when they went out together all the time?

Her mother's voice was quiet. "Tippy, adults need friends just as much as children do. They need people to talk to and share things with. Peter and I have a lot in common. But we're just friends. That's all."

It was as though sunshine broke through clouds, filling Wendy with its brightness.

Her mother continued. "I wonder if any mother anywhere has a daughter who could be so understanding." Her forehead wrinkled. "But why do you think I'm yearning, as you put it, for something?"

Now that was really hard to explain. She couldn't say "Because Ursula Ma'am says so." She settled for something near that truth. "Because when you play your cello it sort of sounds that way."

149

Her mother ran a finger along the edge of the smooth white wood of the bookshelf. "I have so much," she said softly.

Wendy said the word. "Daddy?"

Her mother drew in a deep breath. "Well, that's true. I do miss Daddy." Her eyes were piercing, as though she were trying to see into Wendy. She spoke carefully. "Nobody will ever take Daddy's place. Maybe sometime I'll meet somebody, and I'll love him in a special way. That won't mean I love Daddy less. It'll just be loving two different people, both of them special."

Wendy tried to understand. She really wanted to. And maybe she would, someday. But now it was all murky. Still, she felt in some way airy and—the bears' beautiful word—free.

Her mother bounced to her feet. "It's too nice to stay indoors. Let's walk over to the lake."

Wendy always liked that. It was fun to watch the boats go in and out of the harbor, just feet away from where you were walking on the seawall.

She took her Frisbee, and she was better at it than her mother. Her mother kept fumbling and dropping it. Humans sure got creaky when they got old!

Afterward, they went to the Barkers' for dinner.

Getting ready, changing clothes, Wendy undid her queue and let her hair spread out on her shoulders. It did feel nice, and it looked pretty too. Then she thought about going into the Barkers', and if they all stared and said something about her hair she would surely just die. And someone would too. Because Jeb Barker was just nine-and-a-half months older than she was, and he always called her Windy and grinned in the most revolting way. She absolutely could not stand Jeb Barker. Firmly, she rebraided her hair.

Sunday wasn't bad. At breakfast her mother announced that tomorrow she was going to have to go down to Crawfordsville to approve the color on a book being printed there and she would be getting home very late or not at all. Wendy would have to spend the night with Mrs. Tulippe.

"Aw, Mom," Wendy begged. "Can't I just stay here? Mrs. Tee could come in to say good night."

Her mother wasn't swayed. "No. You're still too young to be without supervision."

"But Mom—"

"No 'buts'."

"Okay." Wendy submitted good-naturedly and finished her French toast. One of these days her mother was going to give in and leave her alone. She sighed. This time it would have been neat, though. She could have spent the whole evening with Otto and Ursula Ma'am.

Her mother seemed to have forgotten about the grounding, and Wendy spent most of the morning and part of the afternoon upstairs. She had more questions.

"I still don't see how the Others are going to know which building to come to."

Ursula Ma'am tried to explain something she did not understand. "They said to turn on the talk thing when they tell us to and to leave it on." Her forehead puckered. "It is the . . . the broad beam."

Wendy understood. "That's what Dr. Corrigan said. They need the beam from your radio to find their entry slot into our atmosphere."

Ursula Ma'am continued. "And they said to make a noise for them. That will be the narrow beam. But how can we make a noise here when we must wait up there?" She gestured upward.

Thinking, Wendy bit her lip. Then she brightened. "My transistor! We can leave it on for them to hear."

"They will follow that noise," said Otto. "And that's how they will find this place among all the others."

Ursula Ma'am was quietly confident. "They will carry us away, and the humans with the fence thing will have to find another place for it."

Wendy was sure that wasn't so! But she didn't try to convince Ursula Ma'am. All the evidence of the past weeks must have made up Ursula Ma'am's mind on the matter of humans and fences. Wendy turned instead to the other thing that was bothering her. "Dr. Corrigan isn't here, yet. You can't just go away without saying good-bye to him."

Otto was troubled by that too. "There will be three sunsets before we must go. Surely he will come."

Oh, if only there were a way to call him and tell him to hurry. But there wasn't. He was still stuck somewhere up on the mountain in the snow. And he wasn't ever going to see Otto and Ursula Ma'am again.

Otto was careful about Dr. Corrigan's advice not to send messages at intervals that humans might predict and so pick up the music. He watched the sun and the shape of the shadows and at random times turned on the set and Ursula Ma'am spoke to the Others.

Wendy listened quietly.

Three more sunsets. Only three.

She went downstairs early in the afternoon, just in time to open the door for Mr. Quirk. She peeked up through her eyelashes. His tie was pumpkin-colored. No need to check his socks. And yet—it was the strangest thing—the familiar sour feelings did not rise in her today. She waited, surprised. No. The feelings weren't there.

He was shrugging out of his coat.

Looking for friendship . . . seeking understanding . . . that's what Otto and Ursula Ma'am had said. But she had known all that last week and it hadn't made a difference in the way she felt. What then? Beautiful violin music? She had known that too.

"This is for you, chum." He thrust a book at her.

It was a book of riddles. She dipped into the middle and laughed at the first one. She followed him into the living room and read it aloud, and the grown-ups laughed too.

It was the strangest thing. Mr. Quirk had changed so much!

She curled up on the sofa and started to read. Her attention was pulled away from the page by the grown-ups' talk.

"—in the lobby just now, and there were two men asking about some bears."

A chill passed through Wendy.

"Bears!!" Her mother set down her glass. "In the city? Oh, you must mean from the zoo."

"No." Mr. Quirk was positive. "Said something about a rare species. They came from the West, these men. Wore cowboy hats. Seems they've been tracking the movements of the animals for weeks now. They heard a rumor from someone about a pilot of a private plane bringing them here. They didn't get the details."

Her mother laughed. "But there's no place for wild animals in this building."

"That's what your doorman told them. Well, they said they were going to recheck their story and they'd be back."

Wendy could have been carved of ice. Should she tell Otto and Ursula Ma'am of this new threat? No, she decided. They would only be scared and there wasn't anything they could do about it. And there were only three more sunsets to wait.

The knowledge lay like a lump of lead in her chest.

She kept the secret until Monday. That's when everything erupted like a volcano.

154

Chapter 16

The next afternoon Wendy had to listen to only nineteen warnings and seven cautions and make fifty promises to Mrs. Tulippe about being in by five. And then she was free to run upstairs. She carried a bagful of gingersnaps with her.

Gingersnaps. The very last gingersnaps Otto and Ursula Ma'am might ever eat.

Hans had indeed come into the apartment that morning to check the TV lead. Otto didn't know exactly what he had done because, of course, he and Ursula Ma'am had stayed in the storage closet.

"Shivering," he assured her, laughing now that the ordeal was past.

"The whole time," added Ursula Ma'am, joining in his laughter.

And so Hans had come and gone and suspected nothing. The antenna was back together, and the bears had been talking with the Others.

There were only two sunsets, now, to wait. Just two.

The three sat cozily around the tree trunk coffee

table as they had that first afternoon, eating ginger-snaps and drinking apple juice. The stones were spread on the green glass. Wendy eyed them. Pleased with herself, she realized she didn't have to be told what was there. White birds gathering at dusk. Otto and Ursula Ma'am had been playing at pebbles "in the bear way."

The book was open on the table, too, to a page of pressed violets. Ursula Ma'am stroked them, smiling the small, secret smile that always came when she mentioned her plans for the distant Brūn. "There will be a place full of these," she said. "A shady place of—"

She never finished.

Noises came from outside. A mechanical whirr. The rattle of metal. The sound of whistling. Startled, they swiveled around to the windows. As they watched, horrified, a window washers' rig descended.

The platform.

Two pairs of boots.

Two pairs of jeans-clad legs.

Even before the rig halted, the men began sweeping sudsy water onto the windows in great curving strokes.

One of the men dropped his brush into a bucket and using a rubber blade wiped a path through the suds. As he did so, his eyes locked with theirs. His mouth sagged. He stood unmoving, the hand with the

156

rubber blade raised, a human statue against the blue backdrop of the sky.

Unable to move, Wendy and the bears stared back.

The man came to life. He gestured wildly to his companion, pointing at them. His words sounded clearly through the glass. "Hey-hey-hey," he stuttered. "Look in there. There's bears in there."

Another section of window was swiped clean and a bearded face leaned forward, eyes shaded from the sky glare. The moment was endless.

The first man's words tumbled out. "The engineer, he said there was some guys looking for bears the other day. Remember?"

The reply was only two words. Two foreboding words. "Let's go."

The rig began to move. Slowly, to the accompaniment of the purring motor, the astonished faces slid downward and disappeared. Rivulets of bubbly water were left running down the window.

From the soles of her feet to the top of her head, Wendy had gooseflesh.

"Humans," gasped Ursula Ma'am. The single word held all the terror of the day of her arrival.

"Ter-r-rible tr-r-rouble," rumbled Otto. The walls of the spacious room seemed to be closing in. "We are tr-r-rapped."

Wendy started breathing again. "Not yet, we aren't! Come on. We've got to go downstairs."

Hastily Ursula Ma'am swept the stones into the valise. She ran for the coats and hats.

Otto unscrewed the antenna and pushed the radio into the suitcases.

"I can carry the antenna," Wendy offered, pushing aside her fear. "Come on. We've got to be quick."

It was like carrying a Christmas tree, awkward but not heavy. She led the way out through the kitchen and shepherded Otto and Ursula Ma'am into the gray cavern of the service stairway.

Otto stopped her before she closed the door. He set down the suitcases and pushed past her, back into the apartment.

"Otto!" Wendy called hoarsely. What was he doing now? "Hey, Otto! We can't waste any—"

He returned on the run, before she finished, carrying the biggest of the pine cones. Grinning crookedly, he presented it to Ursula Ma'am. "For you, love. It was near the talk thing. I knew you would miss it."

"We've got to hurry," Wendy urged, her voice echoing off the cement walls. And shuffling and bumping they got downstairs and into the Devlin apartment.

Upstairs, behind the closed kitchen door, the telephone rang. It rang and rang, the jangle finally blotted out by the rattles and grindings of the elevator rising in its shaft.

The bears were two small islands of desperation. Ursula Ma'am trembled, and so did the flower on her hat. Otto was gray around the lips. Their eyes followed the progress of the unseen elevator as it neared their floor, passed within feet of the door, and ground to a stop upstairs.

Wendy licked her dry lips. "Okay, now," she said, but no sound came out. She coughed and tried again. "Let's go to my room. You can hide in my closet if you need to."

Her bedroom was very different in its blue and white daintiness from the den upstairs, but the storage closet was in the same place. She picked her way past the puzzle, stepped over shoes and books, and flung open the closet door. "Just like Dr. Corrigan's."

The smoky scent of cedar wafted from the closet, inviting the bears to enter. Still wearing their coats, they moved gingerly past a clutter of old toys, a slide projector, red suitcases, music stands, a stack of jig-saw puzzles. They wedged themselves behind a rack of summer clothes.

Wendy waited at the open door, nervously fingering her queue, listening, alert to everything around her. The room was kind of a mess. One by one, she toed the books under the bed. The shoes followed.

In the street below, a siren split the air. And another. And another. They did not pass and fade into the distance. Sirens always passed on to some faraway place. These did not.

Muffled noises came from overhead. A door

slammed. Footsteps thudded on the tiled floors of the kitchen and hall.

Ursula Ma'am's trembling whisper hung in the air of the closet. "Now they are looking for us, the humans."

Otto's words were reassuring, but the burr of his *r*'s gave away his feelings. "They don't know we'r-r-re down her-r-re, love."

"And they don't really know you were upstairs a while ago, either," said Wendy. "The window washers must have said they saw you. But there's nothing up there to prove you were ever really there."

It sounded reasonable. It should have been comforting. But it wasn't. How long must they wait? Would Hans come bursting into the apartment? Would policemen come? And zookeepers?

The drumming of the knocker on the front door sounded through the apartment like gunshots.

Wendy jumped. Her stomach knotted. But she knew what she had to do. She had to answer the door and pretend everything was perfectly okay.

"Someone's at our front door," she whispered. "Don't move till I come back."

The knocker clattered again as she went to answer it. She fastened the night chain and opened the door a crack. Two blue-uniformed police officers stared at her from beyond the chain.

"Your folks home, sis?" asked the younger man.

Wendy shook her head forcefully. Her hand on the doorknob was sweaty.

"We'd like to come in and talk to you," he suggested.

Wendy knew the answer to that one. "I may not let anybody into the house when my mother isn't here," she said primly.

"Let me ask you this." He took out his notebook, ready to write down answers. "Have you seen any b—"

The older man poked him sharply in the ribs. "My partner here wants to know if you've seen anything strange around here this afternoon." He stressed *strange*. The look he directed at the younger man clearly said *Don't scare the kid!*

"Strange?" She repeated the question. Otto and Ursula Ma'am were not "strange."

He picked his words carefuly. "Well, have you seen any—er—wild animals in this building recently?"

Wendy began to get a feel of how to answer the questions. "You mean like lions?" she asked innocently. "Or gorillas?"

"Well, something like that."

"But animals aren't allowed," she said reasonably. "No dogs. Not even a little cat. I don't think they would let a lion or a gorilla in here."

The younger man tried again. "Have you heard any funny noises from upstairs? Growling? Anything like that?"

Wendy's hands had stopped sweating. She had even begun to enjoy herself in a weird sort of way. "Uh-uh. I haven't heard a single growl." She thought back to a long-ago time. "I did hear some banging around up there a couple of weeks ago. Or maybe it was longer ago than that. Maybe it was when Dr. Corrigan—"

The young officer snapped his notebook shut. "Well, thanks, sis. You let us know if anything funny happens around here." He turned away.

The older man smiled kindly. "And you're absolutely right not ever to let strangers into your apartment."

She closed the door and leaned against it. She had never felt so absolutely positively smart in her whole life.

Gently she eased the door open.

The men were waiting for the elevator. "—said there was a kid with them, and the other said there wasn't."

"So maybe there wasn't. But if there was, it wouldn't be that one. She's too little for big-time mischief."

The elevator came to cut off their conversation.

Wendy raced to her room and flung the closet door wide. "You can come out," she announced, smiling broadly. "It was some policemen. I don't think they'll come back—at least not for a while."

The bears stepped into the light, looking relieved.

Otto had another worry. "Even if those humans do not come back, your mother will come. She will see us."

162

"But that's the lucky part." Wendy was glad she could give them some small bit of comfort. "My mother's not coming home tonight. Or if she does, it'll be really late. And anyway, she wouldn't come into this closet. She never does."

The bears shed the hateful coats and shook themselves. Otto regained his color. Ursula Ma'am stopped trembling. Briskly, they set about getting word to the Others.

The ropes of the window washers' rig dangled outside the living room windows. Wendy drew the canary-colored draperies. There would be no more surprises this afternoon if she could help it.

Otto assembled the radio. Ursula Ma'am brought the antenna from the kitchen and screwed it into place. Otto adjusted knobs and signaled readiness.

The first notes from the flute were quivery. A burst of music interrupted. Even Wendy could tell it was a question. Ursula Ma'am replied, her "voice" strengthening as she told the Others what was happening.

Otto leaned forward, his eyes fixed on the radio, listening. Wendy did too, even though she didn't understand. She felt the way she had when she was little and grown-ups spelled things. "Tell me," she wanted to demand. But she didn't. This was grave business.

Otto switched off the radio at last. As one, he and Ursula Ma'am turned to Wendy.

"This dark," he said. "This night. At full dark, when

the glow star has climbed away from its rising place, they will come."

Wendy's heart thumped. Oh, it was happening too fast. But it had to be. Otto and Ursula Ma'am were in danger.

"What's the glow star?" she asked. "And I thought the Others couldn't come until tomorrow."

Otto answered her first question. "The glow star shines warm, like the sun at sunset. We have always known it was important and we have always watched it rise. It is the Others' guide star."

Ursula Ma'am answered Wendy's second question, her voice so soft Wendy found herself watching her lips, lip-reading. "We cannot remain hidden much longer. There is no place for us to go. This dark is not best, but the Others will manage to come."

And then she put a question to Wendy.

"Child, will you show us the way up there?" she asked, lifting her eyes toward the roof. "This dark? This night?"

Chapter 17

Wendy had trouble eating. There was a lump in her throat, and her stomach felt as though it were in the grip of an enormous clutching hand. She pushed her lamb chop around on her plate, poked at her baked potato, and ignored the lima beans.

"My-my-my," fussed Mrs. Tulippe. "We're not touching our food." She tried to be comforting about the thing she thought must be worrying Wendy. "Now dear, there can't be any wild animals in this building. But even if there were, they couldn't get in here. Why, I have four big locks on my door, and . . ." Her voice twittered on, a background to Wendy's thoughts.

It wasn't the "wild" animals that scared Wendy. It was the humans who hunted them. The police officers who had inquired at every apartment in the building. The detectives who had talked to Joe down in the lobby and questioned everyone who came and went. And especially it was the man who just moments ago had tapped on Mrs. Tulippe's door. He had flashed an official-looking card and asked whether she had a "ham" radio or knew of anyone in the building who owned one.

Wendy peeked out from behind Mrs. Tulippe. The man looked ordinary enough, rather like the butcher who had sold her the fish at the Shop and Save. But she knew what he was looking for. Nervously she reached for her queue and stood fingering it.

"Mercy," said Mrs. Tulippe. "What would I be doing with something like that? And why ever are you asking such bothersome questions? It does seem to me we have had quite enough questions in this building for one day."

The man was very polite. "Sorry to trouble you, ma'am. But there's unauthorized broadcasting going on."

Unauthorized broadcasting. Mr. Pick had used those words.

"It's interfering with radio and TV reception. We've been after this for several weeks now. Today we traced it to this neighborhood and maybe to this building. Normally we wouldn't bother people at this time of the day, but—"

But. Wendy knew. Otto and Ursula Ma'am were sending messages almost constantly now. And they would do so until it was time to go up to the roof.

At the mention of interference, Mrs. Tulippe was interested. "Well, I just hope you'll find out who's doing that. Because I've missed three days of 'My Many

166

Lives' already, and I don't know whether Alicia still has amnesia—"

"Yes, ma'am," said the man.

"—and whether John is guilty of murder—"

"Yes, ma'am." The man backed away.

"And whether Hilary has discovered that the maid is really—"

The man looked desperate. "Yes, ma'am." He hurried on before Mrs. Tulippe could continue. "If you'll excuse me, I've got to check the rest of the apartments while we're still getting those signals. Do you know anything about the people at the other end of the hall? I don't get an answer there."

Mrs. Tulippe patted Wendy's head. "Oh, that's Mrs. Devlin, and she isn't at home. The little girl is staying with me tonight."

The man started to tip his hat, only he wasn't wearing one and just touched his forehead. "Thank you, ma'am."

"Dear-dear-dear, what is this building coming to!" Mrs. Tulippe had closed the door. "It used to be such a lovely place," she murmured as she led the way back to the dining room.

A blob of mint jelly slithered off Wendy's fork and onto her sweat shirt. She mopped it up with her napkin.

"I just think someone's had enough sensible food," Mrs. Tulippe said brightly. "Let's us have some apple crunch and ice cream for dessert."

Wendy didn't even finish that. The lump in her throat refused to be swallowed. Fright and excitement and sadness all pulled at her. She felt like the ball in a volleyball game, pitched from hand to hand.

She stirred her ice cream and apple crunch into a messy puddle.

Mrs. Tulippe came around the table and draped an arm around her shoulders. Something besides the bear search, it had occurred to her, might be troubling Wendy. "And your mother will be back tomorrow, dear." She picked up the plates. "Now you just amuse yourself while I tidy up."

Wendy wandered restlessly through the apartment, anxious to be gone. There was nothing she could do, though, until Mrs. Tulippe settled down for the night. Not until the glow star had moved high on its path through the southern sky.

Mrs. Tulippe came into the living room and switched on the TV. Wendy braced herself. The picture scrambled. Of course it would. And the sound burst into pieces.

Regretfully the old lady turned off the set. "I do hope that nice man makes somebody stop whatever they're doing. Well, why don't I read to you? My Theresa always liked that."

Good old Theresa.

And so until bedtime Mrs. Tulippe read aloud, and Wendy sat as quietly as she could, thinking her own thoughts. The hands on the mantel clock moved with wearying slowness.

At last she yawned loudly and Mrs. Tulippe closed the book. "Bedtime for someone," she decided.

The sofa opened out into a bed and Mrs. Tulippe made it cozy with flowered sheets and a soft white blanket. She poured a glass of orange juice and showed Wendy where to find it in the refrigerator. She set out cookies on the kitchen counter, "Just in case you get hungry during the night," something Wendy had never been in her whole life.

She submitted to being tucked in, and chatty Mrs. Tulippe went off at last to her own room. Wendy could hear her in there, clearing her throat from time to time.

She waited as long as she dared, glad for the glowing face of the clock. As the hour hand inched toward nine o'clock—"earth time" as the Others had explained to Otto and he in turn to her—she pulled on her jeans and sweat shirt. Quietly she stuffed the pillows under the sheets. Carrying her shoes, she tiptoed into the foyer.

Feeling in the dim light like a thief opening a safe, she turned the top lock, waiting after the faint click.

Coughs came from the bedroom.

Another lock. *Click*.

Cough-cough-cough.

Tap-tap-tap. Footsteps sounded in the hall. The

169

bathroom light went on.

Wendy froze. Back to the sofa? No! Mrs. Tulippe had to not notice anything wrong in the darkened living room. She just had to. Wendy wedged herself into the shadows next to an antique chair.

Water rushed in the sink, changing pitch as a glass was filled. Pause. The glass clinked on the sink.

Tap-tap-tap. Footsteps retreated down the hall and into Mrs. Tulippe's bedroom.

There were no more coughs.

Wendy turned the last of the locks, slid the door chain out of its groove, opened the door, and slipped through.

The door at the other end of the hall was ajar. She darted to it and slid inside. Otto and Ursula Ma'am were dressed and waiting.

"Got to hurry," rumbled Otto. "Not long now."

Ursula Ma'am clasped and unclasped her paws. "We need that sound the Others will follow here. Then we will be ready.

Hurriedly Wendy put on her shoes and raced to her bedroom. She looked down into the street. Cars still filled the No Parking at Any Time space. What were all those people doing down in the lobby? On second thought, she didn't want to know!

She grabbed her transistor and a brown paper bag and ran to the living room. The transistor was already set at her favorite station. She turned the volume high and placed it next to the glowing red light of the radio.

There. The music, kid music, would be the beacon that pulled the Others straight to the Heywood Arms.

The cheerings were next to the door in the foyer. "Is there room for this?" she asked, offering the paper bag.

Ursula Ma'am took it, her eyes questioning.

"It's lunch," said Wendy. "I made it this afternoon when you were busy. It's peanut-butter-and-jelly sandwiches and apples and bananas and Oreos."

Ursula Ma'am's face softened. She turned to Otto. "It's a dear child," she said softly. "And to think that once I was afraid of it!"

Child. There was a particular gentleness in the way Ursula Ma'am and Otto said that word. It had become an endearment.

But time wasn't to be wasted. "Be quick," Wendy whispered, her hand on the doorknob. "When I open it, run to the door with the light above it. Go up the stairs. If you meet anyone, remember you look like humans in those clothes. Ill be right behind you."

The bears padded to the exit with that astonishing bear speed. Ursula Ma'am, even though she carried the cheerings, moved almost as rapidly as Otto. Wendy eased the door shut and sped after them.

She flew up the stairs, rounding the landings, and almost bumped into the bears outside the door on the twenty-sixth floor. "Not here," she whispered urgently.

"Keep going until the stairs stop."

They sprinted ahead and were waiting when she reached the party room.

"Stay here," she whispered. "I'll make sure nobody's up here."

She inched the door open.

Knee-high night lights around the walls and under the windows gave the room an unnatural, dim glow. She had never seen it like this before.

She stared into each cluster of wicker chairs. Nobody moved in the shadows. Shadowlike herself, she toured the room, peered into the kitchenette, opened the powder room door. Darkness. Nothingness. Emptiness.

She stepped out onto the roof-deck and was alone, absolutely alone, with the city. Great hulks of buildings rose around her, squares of light pasted onto their sides. The lights spoke of humans reading and talking and watching TV—if they could—and getting ready for bed. And not one of them had any idea of what was going to happen tonight on the roof of the Heywood.

In spite of the yellow globe lights that lined the parapet beyond the fence, the deck was spooky. What was it? Something besides the night and the dim light was different. She pushed at her glasses, looking, trying to figure it out. And then she knew. Usually wind blew ceaselessly at this height. Air swept through the fence, around the corners of the party room, sang through the wrought-iron furniture. Tonight no air moved. A wisp of fog drifted through the uneasy calm and erased the upper floors of one of the high-rises.

She hunched her shoulders at the unexpectedly sinister mood of the familiar roof deck and got on with her inspection. It was as deserted as the party room. Relieved, she went inside and conducted Otto and Ursula Ma'am out into the night.

They came timidly, looking around in wonder.

"Real outdoors air," marveled Ursula Ma'am, who hadn't breathed such air, except near windows, in the weeks in Dr. Corrigan's apartment. She took a deep breath.

Otto unbuttoned the long, striped coat. "The last of the hateful fur hider," he gloated. He folded the coat neatly, placed it on the deck, and set the cowboy hat on top of it.

Ursula Ma'am followed his example. She placed the plaid coat beside his and crowned it with the flowered hat.

They shook themselves like playful puppies.

"Almost free," sighed Ursula Ma'am. "Almost!"

That's when the lights went out.

Not just the dimmed lights in the party room.

Not just the roof lights.

The city, the whole city, went black.

The patchwork lights of the high-rises disappeared

and the darkened buildings seemed to press near like lowering giants.

The grid of golden street lights off to the north was wiped out before a wave of darkness that flowed to the horizon. Lights along the Outer Drive paled into nothingness, and now cars could be seen, pushing their lights before them. The red and green of traffic signals ceased their punctuation of the night. The flashing aircraft signal atop the Sears Tower pulled its diamond-hard brilliance into itself and did not reappear.

Ursula Ma'am spoke in the blackness. "And now it's like the mountain," she sighed, and she sounded happy.

"The beautiful blackbird night of the mountain," rumbled Otto.

Wendy did not share their joy. Something was most awfully wrong. A night city was supposed to glitter.

Never had she known such blackness in the city. She had seen something like it only on Grandpa's farm. She reached for Otto and Ursula Ma'am's paws.

As they stood in the raven night, three small, huddled figures, the door of the party room opened. A tall figure stepped out onto the deck. The round beam of a flashlight revealed a pair of boots. It tilted upward and swept their faces. Then that light too went out.

A terrible dread engulfed Wendy.

Chapter 18

The gravelly voice was familiar—low and gruff and reassuring. "It's all right, Wendy. It's Dr. Corrigan. Otto? Ursula Ma'am?"

Everything was going to be just fine! Dr. Corrigan had come. Otto and Ursula Ma'am were going to be able to say good-bye to him after all.

He moved toward them, his voice carefully quiet. "I called this afternoon during my layover in Denver. When nobody answered I was afraid something was going on." The darkness was not so complete as to conceal the folded coats on the deck, the hats, the familiar valise. "Apparently I was right."

They clustered around him, and somehow he managed to touch each of them. They all talked at once.

"Wow! Did things happen around here today!"

"Ther-r-re wer-r-re humans outside."

"They looked at us."

And, of course, none of it made sense to someone who had not been in on the events of the past week. "Wendy? What kind of things?"

She told him. As she spoke, mist sifted through the fence and in passing stroked them with pale fingers of dampness. Wendy didn't notice.

Dr. Corrigan listened to the end, interrupting only to say of the "unauthorized broadcasting," "The government! I was afraid of that. But we had to risk it."

Otto summed up the situation, his burr heavy. "The Other-r-rs said we wer-r-re in danger-r-r. And so they ar-r-re coming, and when the glow star is high they will car-r-ry us away."

They looked eastward, out over the lake. Well above the horizon, in the head of the constellation known as the bull, glowed a reddish orange point of light. Even as they watched, a cloud boiled upward, hiding it.

"Yes, yes. Well." Dr. Corrigan turned up his collar. "Fortunately I got upstairs before the elevators stopped. When nobody was in my place, and nobody answered your door, Wendy, I tried this as my next guess."

Dense fog was rolling in now. It advanced in billowing clouds that both grayed the darkness and thickened the night. There was no current of air, yet the mist moved swiftly, purposefully, drawing ghostly curtains beyond the parapet, shutting out the nearby high-rises.

Silence arrived with the fog, as much a stranger to the city as darkness, and equally eerie. Erased were car sounds, bus sounds, airplane sounds. Not even the haunting bleat of the foghorn—always first to announce the coming of fog to the lake—broke the quiet.

Something was happening to this small place on the earth, to the Heywood. A part of Wendy wanted to turn and run. Another part, the curious part, insisted she stay to see what was going to happen.

The rooftop was brightening, not with a white shine, but with a shifting tint of colors. Where were they coming from? Confused, blinking, nudging at her glasses, Wendy peered upward, to the left, to the right.

The colors deepened, danced in the swirling air, darted restlessly. And now the rooftop was no longer a field of blackness. Flickers of rose, amber, green, amethyst bathed the upturned faces.

With the light came a ripple of sound. It grew into a humming, a humming that did not stop, that blossomed into a tremendous, resounding chord. Something—was it something? Yes, something came into view overhead. Mist curled from it. Was it round? Oval? Impossible to say. Only the glorious colors were a certainty, and the unearthly music, so loud now that Wendy pressed her hands to her ears.

"Slow down!" Wendy's words were swallowed by the throbbing chord. "Oh, it's happening too fast. Not yet. Slow down."

But a course of events that did not involve humankind had been set in motion. Words would not slow them now, or stop them.

The giant object hovered, joining the rooftop to itself as if with bonds of mist and light. The music was reduced to a trembling whisper. A hatch opened in the underside of the great vehicle. A figure moved against the lighted interior.

"Greetings, little friends. In the name of the great Ursus, we of the planet Brūn welcome you." The voice was melodious.

Like a cello! thought Wendy. She remembered that Ursula Ma'am had once spoken in tones not unlike these.

"We are lowering a pod for you," the voice went on. "Move with haste. There is little time, my friends."

A glistening capsule descended to the deck as the voice continued in kindly tones. "You must not bring among us the things of earth to taint Brūn. Leave them behind, little friends. Come as you are, unburdened."

Only at Ursula Ma'am's gasp did the full meaning of those words touch Wendy. "No! Oh, no! Oh, Ursula Ma'am, you've got to take the cheerings!"

"Nothing," intoned the bodiless voice. "It is the rule. It is the law."

At their feet, the butterfly colors of the shifting lights glinted off the brass clasps of the valise. A humble thing, the valise, with its scuffed corners and worn handle. And yet, inside, were the makings of memories sweeter than any Wendy had ever known.

Otto and Ursula Ma'am were, then, never again to admire the lovely symmetry of a pine cone! Never to warm a pebble in their paws! Never to re-create the miracle of fern and violet and oak on some small plot on Brūn!

Bleakly they considered the future.

"Nothing to cheer us."

"Nothing ever-r-r again the same."

The voice overhead spoke. "Little friends, some things are the same. We share the sun with the creatures of Earth—"

"There will be sunsets?" A measure of hope returned to Ursula Ma'am's voice.

"And sunrises!" Otto, quick to find promise in any situation, didn't ask whether there would be sunrises. He knew there would be.

The voice continued. "The stars, we see them from Brūn—"

"The glow star, always ther-r-re!"

"And rain, we have"—rain suddenly sounded a most agreeable thing—"and fog. We have darkness and light. We have warmth and cold."

Silence.

"And we have growing things."

With infinite sadness, Ursula Ma'am looked down at the cheerings. Then she and Otto linked paws. Ursula Ma'am spoke for them both. The soft words were leaden. "We must leave them behind."

And so they made their decision. They would give up the attachments that bound them to their mountain. Not fully knowing what they would find to comfort them on the distant Brūn, they would go.

"We will be fr-r-ree." Otto's voice was strong.

The word, the promise, said it all.

Ursula Ma'am's head lifted. Light returned to her eyes. She stood taller. "Yes. Free."

They took a step toward the waiting capsule.

But weren't they even going to say good-bye? With a ragged intake of breath, Wendy moved to follow them. A hand on her shoulder stopped her. Dr. Corrigan spoke softly. "Let them go happy, Wendy. Let them remember you that way."

Otto and Ursula Ma'am turned.

"Child."

The word hung between them.

"Dear-r-r child."

Wendy swallowed and smiled. She lifted a hand. Words weren't possible.

With a last look over their shoulders, Otto and Ursula Ma'am stepped into the silvery pod. It rose silently as Wendy waved and waved. Then it blacked out the lighted hatch and disappeared inside the spacecraft. Silently the doors slid shut.

Under the skipping lights, Wendy felt small, bereft.

A part of her would be alone all the rest of her life.

Dr. Corrigan spoke. "It's okay, Wendy. They're safe now, and they're doing exactly what they wanted to do."

It was too soon to be comforted by such truths.

It had, finally, all happened too fast.

Trailing streamers of mist, the great craft began to rise. Glorious music filled the night. Played to welcome Otto and Ursula Ma'am to a new free life? Or played in farewell to the two humans who had helped them attain it? Wendy soaked up the music through every pore, to remember, to revive memories of this night.

The music softened. The giant craft began to spin. The colors whirled about Wendy and Dr. Corrigan, mixed, paled, and the light turned white. More swiftly than one would have believed possible, the ship rose upward. A cloud enclosed it. The light dimmed and died, and darkness shrouded the rooftop.

A wind came up. The mist beyond the parapet thinned to reveal the surrounding high-rises. Points of candlelight gleamed in some of the nearer windows.

The rooftop came alive with its accustomed song as the wind whipped through the fence and around the corners of the party room. In passing, it dried Wendy's face. At her feet, atop a neatly folded red plaid coat, the stick-up flower on a red hat bobbed in the moving air.

City sounds returned.

Buses grumbled. Car horns beeped. Sirens, from all directions, wailed, growing louder, louder, louder as they drew closer to the Heywood.

As abruptly as they had died, the globe lights on the parapet returned to life. Wendy blinked in the glare. Brightness spilled from the windows of high-rises. Street lights picked their way northward to the horizon. Far downtown, the airplane beacon on the Sears Tower stabbed the night with its blue-white beam.

"Look." Dr. Corrigan pointed out over the lake to where several clouds hung suspended. Wendy squinted. Did one of them give off the shifting glow of opals?

"I wonder," she said, "if sunsets on Brūn are like sunsets here, and if the growing things are—are—"

Dr. Corrigan dug a folded handkerchief from his jacket and offered it. "We'll never know. But remember —we don't know what beauties are waiting for Otto and Ursula Ma'am, either."

Behind them, the party room door burst open.

"Wendy!"

It was her mother.

"I have been out of my mind with worry. What in the world have you been up . . ." The words faded as she took in Wendy's tear-stained face, the folded coats on the deck, the cowboy hat, the hat with the stick-up flower, the valise. "Darling, are you all right?"

Hastily, Wendy reassured her. "Hey, Mom, wait'll

I tell you what happened." The cross-her-heart promise was over. She could tell about Otto and Ursula Ma'am without breaking her word.

She remembered the tall figure beside her. "Mom, this is Dr. Corrigan." She hiccuped. "He doesn't wear go-along socks," she added.

There was a startled silence. Then her mother's head went back and she laughed her prettiest-mother-any-where laugh. Shakily Wendy joined in. It felt peculiar, and good, to laugh after the fear and unhappiness of the past half hour.

Dr. Corrigan's craggy face was a study in bewilder-ment. Momentarily he looked admiringly at Mrs. Dev-lin. Then, dazed, lifting his pants legs a few inches, he inspected his hiking boots. Not an inch of sock showed. "I—I don't understand."

Mrs. Devlin turned pink. "Oh, I'm so sorry!" She tried to explain. "Wendy gauges people by their socks." But it was beyond explanation and she gave up.

She came to Wendy and dropped an arm around her shoulders. Her relief over, it was time for serious-nes. "Something told me I should get a plane out of Indianapolis tonight instead of waiting until tomorrow, and I was right. You've got some tall explaining to do, young lady. How often have I told you to stay off this roof?"

"Mom, I—"

"And at night!"

"But Mom, I—"

"And how could you play such an unkind trick on nice old Mrs. Tulippe? She's downstairs having a breakdown."

Well, back to grounding. Back to memorizing *Alice in Wonderland*. She would be lucky to get out of prison before Thanksgiving.

Dr. Corrigan spoke to her mother. "Try not to be too hard on her. Let her tell her story. It's an incredible tale, but I'll back her up on it."

Wendy shifted restlessly. Her foot touched the valise. Kneeling, she opened the clasps. The first thing her fingers touched was long, knobby in the way a slender branch is knobby, with fingering holes worked into it. Ursula Ma'am's flute.

Inside the party room, the elevator doors opened and a crowd of police officers spilled out. Lights blazed, casting oblongs of brightness onto the deck, illuminating the three figures who stood there.

Wendy shuddered. There was going to be an awful lot of talking. She moved nearer Dr. Corrigan. Without glancing down, his eyes on the police officers, he thrust a hand in her direction. She slid hers into it and it closed around her fingers, big and warm and secure.

Sandwiched between her mother and Dr. Corrigan, she raised her eyes to the sky. There were thousands of stars. Millions. Billions. Among them, moving swiftly away from the earth, were two not overly large, blue-eyed bears. And they were free.

Wendy formed words silently. "Hey, Otto, good-bye." And, "Good-bye, love."

The old wood of the flute was satiny in her hand. And, yes, it was comforting.

"Thank you," Wendy whispered, stroking the wood with her thumb. "Thank you."

MS READ-a-thon— a simple way to start youngsters reading

Boys and girls between 6 and 14 can join the MS READ-a-thon and help find a cure for Multiple Sclerosis by reading books. And they get two rewards — the enjoyment of reading, and the great feeling that comes from helping others.

Parents and educators: For complete information call your local MS chapter. Or mail the coupon below.

Kids can help, too!